1

Contents

Prologue

When an angelic woman who looked as if she was made of light appeared to a man on his one-hundredth birthday, he was surprised by her question.

"Have you heard of a man who goes by the name MG?"

He looked as if she was joking; there were millions of people on Earth, and a million of them could have had the initials MG. When the angel told him that this man was important for the safety of humanity and the world, he wondered why she was talking to him. The angel said.

"In your life of solitude and wisdom, have you ever noticed the same face and the same initials in all your search for knowledge?" When she realised she sparked a schema, she smiled and gave him a task.

"Find this man and warn him." she vanished.

As a boy, this old man recalled his grandfather telling him the stories his great, great grandfather told about a man who lived at the North Pole and came down once a year. The man never aged. He looked like a boxer who fought for gold back when the Olympics were a thing for unity and sportsmanship rather than glory and pride. When the man was a teenager, he started reading to see if there was any truth to this myth. When he was an adult, he took a vow of solitude when he discovered that his grandfather was on to something, that a family lived around the world and looked the same. There were statues taken by tourists and images of a face in the background of portraits. It wasn't until the man was in his 80s that he saw the face appear again in the media. Yet he never believed the real truth until now.

After two and a bit years of connecting dots, this man, now one hundred and three, put together the truth, that there was something special about this man, and if the angel told him to warn him, he had to get a message to him. The old man wrote a letter after discovering where he lived and looked around his home of solitude and hoped that he would come in time. While searching for him, he discovered the reason the angel came. He saw what people were capable of, and if this man had some part in preventing it, he didn't need an answer to a question he wanted to ask. The man that the angel wanted to warn needed to hear the truth from his own lips.

While this was all happening, a young woman with hair the colour of the night was in a kitchen of a small home. Washing up after feeding her husband and three children, she looked at her growing belly and sighed. She was miserable and felt trapped and helpless. She thought back several years when she first arrived on the island and saw the statue carved from solid rock. It was of a man holding a stick; apparently, that was the first person that showed kindness to the locals. He defended their ancestors, the first Leader of the Island. However, she didn't see any kindness. She knew that soon she would have another child and hoped that all four of her children would grow up in a world full of kindness.

Meanwhile, a fair-haired young lady was coming up with a way of moving loads of books, magazines, comics and art such as paintings, drawings and photographs that she had collected over the decade. She moved into a large building that she designed and built to hold the books and writings on shelves and hang the paintings in a gallery. She had this ambition to learn about the past and teach it to others, and she started to dig into the past. This woman gathered enough information on the past, and she was fascinated by the stories of a family of fighters in the time of 800AD Rome. She was hooked by the family that travelled around a country and the story behind the painter that worked alongside one of the greatest. She only knew what she had written from her research and was intrigued by the one thing that kept popping up throughout history: the initials M G.

The angel appeared to the man one last time, and this time she looked quite pleased; she smiled and stood over his bed. She arrived minutes after he had fainted from an episode of the heart. The man heard something that shocked him and also that made total sense. She looked at the wise old man and spoke gently as if she was his mother.

"You got more than you expected, and now you have many questions. Let me tell you a story. You will not find these in the books you have read, and this story hasn't finished yet."

The man closed his eyes and listened to her talk, and this story was about the Legacy of the Immortal. She started from the very beginning with the Early Life of a Miracle Child.

Early Life of Miracle Child

The year was five hundred, and Clovis, the founder of the Frankish state, conquered most of France and Belgium, converting his people to the Catholic religion. Early in the year, a couple hid from the marching troops and expressed their forbidden love, for their families were rivals and forbade them to see each other. Three weeks after that day, Judith, the daughter of Adelaide, found herself sick and very weak. They called a healer in and asked Judith questions that she refused to answer before her mother. When the mother left, Judith freely replied, "The last interaction I had with the outside world was three weeks ago with the love of my life." The healer said, "Then you might be with child, but we cannot know until your body shows signs. You can come to me in two weeks' time."

The next two weeks were slow and painful with Judith staying in bed, hiding the news the healer gave her, her mother asked what it was, and Judith replied, "An illness, mother, it should go away in a month's time." Nevertheless, when two weeks ended later, and Judith was feeling sore and tender in her belly, she went to the healer and asked, "How bad is it, for can you tell if I am with child?"

The healer (a female) felt under the garments, and when Judith jumped at the touch of her breasts, she nodded and replied, "Yes dear, you are with child, and shall I inform your parents?"

"No, we must not, for if they find out, then both the baby and I will surely die, I must inform my lover, and then we can sail across the border to seek sanctuary."

"But that trip could take days, weeks even, and you will not manage alone. You must take family."

"Sorry, healer, but once I fell in love with my family's rival's son, my life was given a death sentence. I must flee to the Island in the north and seek Sanctuary. Please tell my mother that I died of the illness I had a week after writing to you telling you where I am."

"If that is your wish, my dear, I will do so."

With that, Judith ran to find Baxter and tell him of the news, Baxter Gelan was over the moon with the news, and they fled to the shores of what will be the town of Oostende and grabbed a boat. Baxter, after packing a bag of food, started rowing out. They started rowing as the sun began to set. The journey took a day, eleven hours and twelve minutes, but it felt like weeks. After twenty-four hours of rowing and running out of food, they soon fell asleep and drifted with the current. When they woke up, they were cold and wet and off course. They both rowed towards Britannia, and after another 12 hours, they arrived at what will be Hastings. They landed and found themselves a home.

A few weeks later, they recovered from their trip. Judith was now nine weeks pregnant. She started to make crazy demands and was screaming and crying one minute and laughing the next. This lasted two weeks, and Judith was complaining about her breasts. Another four weeks later, Judith's belly was visible under the loose garments. She was bleeding from the nose and had trouble eating with swollen gums. It was Friday the sixteenth of June when they found themselves a means to get married. On the first of July, when seventeen weeks pregnant, Judith suffered from nightmares of demon children. They got married on the second, and Judith became Judith Gelan. After the wedding, they found an inn, and Baxter made love to her, lowering her libido.

Soon it was August, and Judith had growth in her breasts. Her belly was larger, and her back was aching; she was around twenty-three weeks when she started to complain about the pain. After another week or so and the pain was throughout her body, she was screaming and wishing it would just stop; the bed they had was uncomfortable in the house Baxter built with the boat and spare parts. They were sleeping on the floor, and Baxter worked with the bread to make his money. The kicks were slow and steady and were not as painful as the aches in the back, legs and arms. After another month of troubled sleeping and pains from the changing body, Judith looked healthy with perfect hair, skin, and nails. Then, on the night of the twenty-eight of September, the east wall of their house collapsed. Judith was screaming as the baby kicked inside her, she was now thirty weeks pregnant, and blood was coming from above the stomach. A piece of wood was sticking out of her chest where the wall fell from wind and rain. The wound was open, and the splinters were heading toward the bloodstream. Baxter ran for the healers the minute the wall collapsed. The healers were doing their best, and after countless hours, the wood was out.

Two months after the accident, Judith was lying on the straw bed with water next to her and the female healers telling her to push. She counted forty-one weeks, and the baby was holding on as if it did not want to leave. After a long night, at sundown on the twelve of December, a silent baby was born, but that was not right. Where was the crying? The healers checked the baby and, after long hours, finally spoke, "The baby is dying, his body is shutting down, for he is dying on the inside!" they sounded sincere, and with no money, they were looking at the baby.

Judith said, "Well if he is going to die, we better give him a name. What do you think, Baxter?"

"I think we should name him Harding as he will be brave and come back from this."

"How long until he dies?" Judith asked the healers.

"Three days," they replied, showing all signs of sadness. They left saying, "there is nothing we can do."

The next morning around midday, an old man with a beard and scars appeared and said, "I am a great healer, a man of magic; I can cure your child, but to do so, I need his blood."

Baxter asked, "How will you heal him?"

"I will give him power from beasts, I will combine his blood with the blood of a dragon, the essence of a sea star and a scale from a fish of life, and he will recover."

With those words, Baxter allowed the man to prick the baby's skin. He returned and gave him a needle that night, and the baby went to sleep. "When he wakes, he will cry for the first time."

The baby was having trouble breathing, Judith kept watch of the baby that night, and when the sun rose, they heard a sound around the house. The baby was crying, Judith was relieved, and Baxter was thrilled. Then Judith said, "His name will be now Michel Harding Gelan, for he was a gift of God to still be with us."

And for the next few years, they watched Michel grow up and noticed that he was different and remembered the medicine man's words. "He will be different when a human's cell dies. It takes a long time to grow a replacement. Michel's will recover and replace way faster. It will be like there never was a dead one." It was true; every scratch, every bruise was recovered in a heartbeat, and every broken bone was recovered in a day. Judith and Baxter were both in their twenties, and watching him grow made them realise that there would be a day when he would live beyond their age, which would cause him to mourn. Knowing that they went to their bedroom, wrote a letter, and placed it in a hollow bone of a horse, the letter read. "To our son, if you are reading this, you have lived a long life and are still living, remember that the Lord placed you on this earth to live for a reason. The world would have changed, but you remain the same. You will be remembered but promise us you will remember the way of the Father, and you will not live in pain and suffering, but to the fullest, you can do, Signed your parents." They created a necklace and placed it in a box. They then wrote their last requests and continued to watch their son grow.

On Michel's fifth birthday, they celebrated for life to this point was a battle, but Michel suffered no disease, no wound that killed him. A few years later, Michel was eight, and with that, his parents had turned thirty, and they were on the edge of the bell curve, for they were strong. Judith didn't take another risk, so Michel was their only son, and they loved him all their heart. Times were tough, and the food was low, but they survived off fish, and by luck or by fate, Michel ate the poisonous fish and survived while his parents had the safe ones. By the time he was thirteen, they had praised the Lord that they were alive to be there for him. They were getting older and feared they would not see him become a man. With their risky lifestyle, hiding the truth from the rest of the townfolk was becoming a nightmare. With them working by the sea, they were far away as they could get but were still getting strange looks, and after another six years, they finally were getting old, and their bodies were dying.

In the streets, Michel was trying to get some fish from the Fishmonger when the man refused. Michel pushed past the man and reached for some fish, only the Monger grabbed his arm and threw him into the sand. Michel spat sand out of his mouth and dusted the grains from his cheeks. He stood behind the man, snarling and panting. He punched him in the ribcage. The Fishmonger groaned and spat on the ground before grabbing the hook from one of the boats and stabbing Michel in the chest. He pulled it out and said: "Guess you will all die now." However, to Michel's surprise, he was healed after the bleeding stopped; a few minutes later, he was scar-free. He ran home to see his parents lying in bed and cried, "Mother, Father, I was dying, but I was healed; why was that so?"

"You are special, son. Remember that you cannot get injured for a long period of time. You will grow strong and be an example to the people who believe in Satan. You will do great things, but listen before you do great things. You will be tested, you will have to lie to survive, and the Lord will forgive you for that. You will pretend to be another man in order not to be called a demon. You will see great things, so remember that we love you. Take this box and wear the necklace proud. It will be your heirloom. Make us proud."

Michel cried and turned to his father, and Baxter spoke with a cough draining his voice, "Son, you are a Gelan, you are Harding and Michel, Brave and Gift of God, do us proud and never forget that title."

Michel's parents died the next month in the harsh winter, for during the nights, the fire couldn't keep them warm, and they started to feel drowsy. During the days, the coughing got worse, and their speech was going. Michel fed them and did the jobs, but the food could not ease the cough. Michel woke up to hear the parents coughing up blood, and he watched the life fade from their eyes before the sunset. He buried their bodies and wrote on their tombs. He then found a house on the coast away from the town and lived alone.

Time passed, and soon Michel was celebrating his thirtieth birthday, and he began to notice that he was slowing down. He was not growing old with age, his skin was as healthy as always, and his hair was not getting any greyer. He lived in the house for the next ten years, rarely going out and watching, as he did not change. His face stayed the same, and so did his skin. No scars, not even a sign of him being forty, made him remember what his parents said the day he asked the question. ""You are special, son. Remember that you cannot get injured for a long period of time. You will grow strong and be an example to the people who believe in Satan. You will do great things, but listen before you do great things. You will be tested, you will have to lie to survive, and the Lord will forgive you for that. You will pretend to be another man." Therefore, he walked out the door, entered the streets, and bought some food. The Fishmonger's son saw him and said, "Hey, your face is familiar. Have we met?" The man was in his 50s, and his hair was grey, and Michel lied, "Name's Matthew Gelan, my father spoke of you, he died and said 'Never buy fish from the traitor,' my mother found him dying on the streets when he was nineteen, and they moved in together on the hill, that's my home now."

Indicating the house where he lived all his life.

"My father passed away, more like drowned. Guess we are both fatherless, sorry for what my father did; he was greedy." Michel forgave the man for his father's deeds knowing in his heart that the man does not know that he is Michel.

This happened every few decades. Michel grew old and pretended to be his own son; by the time he was pretending to be Michel the fourth, Heraclius became Emperor in Constantinople. The Persian Empire tried to invade the Byzantine civilisation, which became their history.

He lived through the battle between the Persians and the Byzantine civilisation and heard about the reclaiming of the cross. He was Michel the sixth when Heraclius died in six hundred forty-one. Even was there as Michel the seventh saw the downfall of Byzantine to the Arab nation. Michel grew tired and old pretending to be his own son and travelled east out of the country only to get as far as Thrace when stopped by the Arab Nation during their takeover attempt in six hundred seventy-seven CE. After surviving the arrows and rocks, Michel picked himself up and returned to his home on the hill as Michel the tenth. Sick of being Michel, the next time he came out of hiding, he was Matthew the second in the year seven-ten, ten years after Benedictine missionaries completed the conversion of Anglo-Saxon Kingdoms. Michel, as Matthew went to the church and prayed. Then he went to the graveyards, looked at the tombstone that was about the length of a coffin and on it was a list of all Michel's lies, every name he pretended to be and their corresponding wives, all without a date of death. Above their names was a single line, 'the Gelan family will be remembered'. Then he went to his real parent's tombs and waited until dark. He then got out a candle and prayed.

"Father, I was told I was to suffer, but I have lived for two hundred years, and I am looking at my parent's tombs. I have seen bloodshed and my generation die over and over again. If you wish for me to continue, please send me a sign that I am doing the right thing, give me a sign, for Father, I am becoming a lie, my real name was lost decades ago, and all I am is an echo of my true self. Please show me that I am meant to live on."

Seven years after that prayer, the Arabs were defeated by Byzantine Emperor Leo the Isaurian, using what he called 'Greek Fire', a combination of sulphur, naphtha, and quicklime. They started to reconquer Asia Minor and take their ground as a civilisation and Michel started to see trouble as he became Matthew the fourth in the year seven hundred and forty and watched the name of Christ vanish from the Byzantine civilisation. He goes there by boat with the fishermen and arrives months later on the coast. Sixty years under Matthew the sixth hears word that Carolus Magnus has succeeded after his father and that he accepted Alcuin of York into the area to teach. Michel leaves for the Frankish area and asks under the name of Matthew the seventh to help teach the people. He helped at the school for a decade, went into hiding around the year seven hundred and ninety, arrived at the turn of the century as Matthew VIII, and got word that Charlemagne might be getting crowned emperor before the end of the year.

With that news, Michel Gelan headed to Italy to the centre of Rome to become a Roman citizen and help spread the word of Christ by reading the scriptures and teaching anyone that listened. He left at the end of spring after the Celebration of Easter and walked towards the border, fearing no death or illness, his wounds from his bare feet healed, and the dust in his blood released itself when an animal attacked him. He walked all day and night; he arrived when the day was long on June 24th and asked for Sanctuary. When they asked for his name he lied and said, "My name is Maximus Gladius, I have travelled far to find a way to earn money is there any way to do so?"

When in Rome, Act like a Roman

"Well Maximus, we do have spots in the Colosseum to replace people who have just lost, if you think you are strong, sign up, and if you win, you will be rewarded with riches."

"Riches sounds good. How do you earn these riches?"

"Fight, of course," the Roman guards said, giving him a hand to sit upon his horse. Michel frowned at the sight of him battling and revealing his true nature, but instead, he smiled and said, "Well, then fight I must do. When can I sign up to be a part of the Roman Empire?"

"Once you win your first fight, you can ask to be a citizen. If you lose your first fight, then I guess you are a citizen but a dead one," the guard laughed at the idea, and Michel hid his worried face. Finally, after three hours of horseback riding, Michel arrived in the Great City of Rome. Michel stepped off the horse and passed the walls at the border. Once through, a man gave him a look over and said, "Give him a band, if he is a fighter, the town must know, so what name are you fighting for?"

"Christ and Gelan."

"Gelan, strange name. Who are they?"

"They were a family friend," Michel replied and received a horsehair and metal dog tag. The tag said "Maximus Gladius:

Fighter", and Michel smiled at his new name and continued to follow the guard to the Inn and was given a room. In a week, he would be fighting. It was July first when Michel stepped into the arena as Maximus.

Maximus stood in the arena and looked around at the crowd of men and soldiers. Then out came his opponent, a man one and a half his height. Maximus looked at his competition and smiled. However, when Maximus saw the sword he held, his smile turned straight. A sling and a net Maximus received for a first-timer. Closing his eyes for a second, Maximus prayed to the Lord for advice, and when he opened his eyes to find himself thrown into the air, a story from the Bible came to his mind. Maximus landed hard on a rock, and the blood stopped the minute the wound was open. Acting fast, Maximus used his sleeve to cover the open wound that was now a small hole to hide it from the audience, and he then grabbed some small stones. Using the sling, he tossed the rocks towards the giant, and as he staggered forward, Maximus used the net to trip him over. The giant fell forward, face-first into the same rock that injured Maximus. The giant was out cold. The leader gave a thumbs-up and shouted down into the arena, "Use his sword, finish him off!"

Maximus yelled back up so the crowd could hear, "Never shall I kill; this man fought honourably, he lost, but he is not going to die because of that."

The Leader chuckled and said, "Very well, he will fight alongside you against the reigning champion."

They took both of them to a cell, dragged the giant and when they were placed into a cell, Maximus used water to wake him up. The giant groaned, "Either I am dead, and you died in the next fight, or you are stupid enough to let me live."

"Why stupid, you fought well?"

"I lost after a killer toss; you should be dead, weakling. How come you are not?"

"That is my curse by both our Gods for me to live on." Maximus removed the sleeve to reveal no scar. "I cannot die from battle unless it cannot be removed. I am telling you this because we will be in battle with the reigning victor in tomorrow's fight, and you might not survive!"

The giant muttered, "I am Octavius, last son of my father Felix, I have won three fights, one less than this victor, and if I had beaten you, I would have been released. So, he doesn't scare me."

"In that case, we better plan for a victory, for I cannot pretend to be lucky thrice."

"Plan we shall do. What do you have in mind?" Octavius asked.

"Depends on how strong this Victor is?" Maximus replied.

"He is ten-foot-tall and is twice as strong as me, I am small, and you are tiny compared to him."

"So, he is twice my size; I guess that means I can go low. Now I have a plan!"

Using the sword, Maximus drew three figures and spoke in a low whisper so the guards could not hear, "You will throw me with the net at this Giant, and he will knock me aside. I will fall and lie down and wait for him to wear tired. You will fight and block until he is tired. Let him knock your sword away once he is weary and let it fall towards me. Then I will hit his ankle, and you will punch him in the jaw, and that will finish him off."

"You think it will work?" Octavius asked, looking sore and worried.

"If my years of training were for battle, then yes, it should work."

"Years?"

"Too many to count. Remember, I cannot die!"

After a long sleep, Maximus and Octavius woke up and got ready for battle. "Your fight is at sunrise; you have an hour to prepare for battle and make peace with your maker!"

After the hour, Maximus stood in his little armour, and Octavius was holding his sword. "You will be facing Atticus, the Victor," The Leader announced to the crowd and mainly to them. The ten-foot giant stood his ground and bellowed across the arena, "You are both weak compared to me, prepare to fail and die!"

He charged, taking average strides but compared to Maximus's, they were long. Maximus jumped and held his net like he was ready to charge when Octavius grabbed him and threw him right at Atticus as they planned. Just as Maximus hoped, he has pushed aside with one hand. Maximus covered his face, rolled, hit the wall and played injured. Octavius jumped forward and blocked the club with his sword. The sword and club clashed, metal on wood, and the sound of splitting wood echoed the arena's walls. For the next five minutes, it was sword blocking club or club hitting sword.

Maximus got up on all fours, crawled over to Atticus, and while he was distracted, signalled Octavius. The club hit the sword, and Octavius loosened his grip on the hilt and let the sword fly to the ground. Atticus was huffing and puffing; the sweat reflected the sun, he was worn out, but the giant was full of energy, for he conserved his energy by taking big strides and long jumps to dodge while the Victor ran to attack. Maximus picked up the sword and sliced the ligament in Atticus's ankle as he hopped in pain; Octavius swung his closed fist and punched him clean in the jaw. The unbalanced Victor dropped his club onto the uninjured foot and fell backwards, landing on the pile of rope, which was the net. He landed unconscious. The leader gave the thumbs up and declared, "The winners are Octavius and Maximus. Octavius is free to leave. Maximus you have two fights left before you can go!"

Maximus walked over to Octavius and handed the sword over. Without warning, he then used the club to knock Octavius senseless, saying "That is for throwing me at him," as he helped him down and as he lost consciousness, Maximus whispered, "You are free, and my secret is safe."

Maximus went into the inn's ward and saw Octavius being treated. They looked at him and said, "if you want a drink, the ale is over there. I think you need some. This was the second time you were thrown around!"

"Guess I better grow roots for my third fight." Maximus joked and went up to his room. After a fortnight off, Maximus was given an easy challenge for his next two fights. Maximus used the club to win the next two fights and was awarded freedom. Maximus left and found a hut on a hill; it was old and abandoned, and he placed a tombstone, engraved the words "Beloved wife", and then lived there for twenty years. During this time, Charlemagne died without leaving competent successors to continue the glory of the Carolingian dynasty. His sole surviving son, Louis, the Pious, divided his inheritance between his own three sons, who engaged in civil war. Scandinavian Vikings, Hungarians and Muslims invaded Charlemagne's united realm during the civil wars in which Maximus sat back and watched agelessly and never changing.

When it was autumn in the year eight hundred twenty, Michel walked out the doors with new clothes and the same club and walked towards the wall surrounding the great city. The guards spotted Michel and shouted, "Who comes to the gates?"

"My name is Marcus Gladius, son of Maximus. I am here to fight for his honour, the money he earned was used in the twenty years when I went from teen to man, and I will now fight!"

He received a necklace with his new name and was placed into the ring. His previous fighters from twenty years ago, all grew old, it was a new decade, and Marcus was ready to earn money. They notified him to win six in a row, which started next week. Sleeping in the inn and practising for the fight,

Michel, as Marcus, was ready for the battle. He walked in after the week, and saw the Leader still sitting on the throne, who looked at Marcus.

"You look like your father; will you fight like him?" The leader spoke to Marcus.

"I was bequeathed his club that he won; I will do it proudly." Michel lied and then waited for his opponent.

Michel's opponent was average in ability, and after battling for over an hour, he stood bruised as they announced him the winner.

This would last two months, Marcus fighting, earning the crowd's respect, and then he would leave and go to the hut and hideaway for twenty years. During those twenty years, the Arabs conquer Crete, Sicily, and Sardinia in only a year. Deciding to leave Rome, travelling as Marcus, Michel saw all of Italy, including Leonine City

When the Muslim Arabs invaded Rome and stole all the gold and silver in St. Peter's Basilica, Michel decided to change his name to Magnus. In response to the looting, Pope Leo IV started building the Leonine walls of the Leonine City, the year after, in 847, it took six years to build - which Michel helped build as Magnus. When Michel returned to Rome and his hut on the hill seven years later, he was clean-shaven, hair cut short and wearing new clothes.

It was soon eight hundred sixty when Michel arrived at the Colosseum. The Leader's son greeted him and said, "You must be Marcus's grandson. You have the same face, same club and even the same silly necklace they wore, and where is your grandfather, the keeper of the record of six victories in a row?"

"He is buried in the hillside. Along with his wife, parents, and son, who died just after I was born."

"Pity to hear that. Will you fight in their name?"

"Theirs and Gelan's, we haven't heard from them in Hastings since they were told we were gladiators."

"Here is your tag. My Uncle is the Leader now. My father died five years ago."

"I am sorry to hear that; I shall put on a show for the new Leader then." Michel then placed on the new tag and walked toward the Colosseum. Arriving there, he saw the new Leader and realised that he might not be able to convince him to let the losers live on. Magnus had to wait a whole season before he could fight someone allowing the fighters a chance to surrender. When it was time to fight, he walked into the arena and saw his opponent, it was the grandson of Atticus, and he looked angry. "YOUR FAMILY MADE my GRANDFATHER look like a JOKE! I will tear you apart!"

"Have fun trying", Michel muttered under his breath and faced the grandson.

"What was that, Gladius!"

"I said, you can try," Michel lied and then charged with the weapon that once belonged to their family.

Atticus the third dodged and kicked Magnus in the back and into a wall. When Magnus hit the wall, he used his arms to push off and jump the wall. Walking on the edge, Magnus got out of range and then picked up a rock and tossed it at Atticus's skull. Atticus used his sword to block the attack and then charged. Jumping over with legs apart, Magnus managed to land behind him and kick him in the back like a horse making Atticus fall over the wall. That made Atticus furious, and he picked up a huge piece of rock and tossed it at Magnus, Magnus jumped aside, and the rock shattered, causing pieces of dust to enter the bloodstream. Magnus covered the healing wounds using rags from previous battles and then limped away, pretending to be injured.

Falling for the trap, Magnus waited for the right time, and when Atticus charged, sword high, ready to cut the shoulder blade. Meanwhile, Magnus was using the club as a cane, and when the shadow of Atticus was over his, Magnus raised the club and hit Atticus straight in the nose; the sword dropped, missing his feet by inches, and Atticus staggered backwards in pain. Then Magnus turned around and saw Atticus on the ground screaming mercy. The Leader's brother (the new leader) gave the thumbs up and said, "Your choice, kill or let him fight another day."

"Let him try again when he recovers from a broken nose!" Michel walked away, and as he did, suddenly a blade was sticking into his back and inside his stomach. It missed the main organs, but it was still in Magnus's body. Pulling it out, dust and tiny rocks fell from the open wound and then Magnus ran from the arena. Days later, he returned in new clothes and with no scars. The new Leader's nephew saw him walk towards the wall and said: "Are you, Magnus?"

"Yes."

"How did you survive the sword; Atticus was forbidden to fight after that dirty trick?"

"I am a quick healer, I found some plants to keep me alive, but I must still fight in the arena, my sister is dying, and I need money to support her."

"Why don't you go to her?"

"I must fight for her, she was born deaf, and I think she will not make it for another year. This is my last chance to get money. Will you allow me entry?"

"Of course, you still have five fights left to be given freedom. The Leader thinks you are dying somewhere. I shall tell him the news."

Magnus arrived at the inn and saw the other fighters stare, and then one said, "If I have to fight, you will do me the pleasure of killing me, I am dying, and a death in the arena is better than a death of an illness."

"I will do no such thing if you happen to die. It will be not my fault but yours."

Sure enough, that weekend, Magnus was up against the dying man. Magnus saw that he was already sweating; deciding to make something certain, he asked: "How many have you won?"

"I have won five, and I know your family has never lost yet."

Magnus had two options, lose and face the possibility of his secret being known or win and then make the man die with illness and humiliation. Magnus turned to the Leader and asked: "What if there is a draw and neither wins?"

"If you are both down, it will be called a draw, and both will be announced winners!"

Under his breath, Magnus muttered, "That makes it easier."

As Magnus charged, so did his opponent. When they were close, Magnus whispered: "We will both lose that way you and I will be able to get out, and if you die, it will be a free man and a champion."

"That is if you don't kill me first", and he swung his sword at Magnus's chest. Magnus dodged and then used the club to hit him in the stomach after a couple of hits from both sides. Magnus found a way to win; he tossed the club into the air and tackled the rival to the ground and punched him in the jaw, and said, "When the club falls, both of us will lose", and then knocked him out just before the club hit Magnus in the back of the head. Magnus woke up in the Inn hospital to hear that his opponent was released and was given his money and freedom. Magnus smiled and asked, "When is my next fight?"

"Next week," replied the innkeeper and said, "You better rest. You were lucky the club didn't kill you."

"Guess I have a knack for staying alive," Magnus replied and walked back to his room. He went to his chest and pulled out the box his mother gave him, and inside were tokens of his old lives. There were the two other tags for the fights. There were trinkets from his old home and the ones he lived in. Magnus looked out the window and prayed, "Father in heaven, if I am to walk this earth alone, please show me which way to go."

"Excuse me," a shy feminine voice said from behind the door. Magnus opened the door to see a lady in her thirties dressed in fancy garments. She smiled seductively, "I am here to entertain the family of reigning champions; my family is paying me to entertain winners."

"Really, and what is the job description?"

The attractive woman shut the door and dropped the top of the dress to reveal her beautiful body. Magnus gulped at the sight of a pretty woman; for three hundred years, he had not seen someone as beautiful as her. For the next four days, she stayed in the room. After four days of close intimacy, Magnus felt the love, but then he remembered something, just as her nails (which had grown in four days) scratched his skin. The scratches healed. He turned to see her lying in bed next to him. Magnus stepped out of bed and said, "I can't do this. This is wrong. You have to leave."

"Why? Is it because you have a son and sister?"

"That's ...right."

"Or is it because you have a secret weapon during the battles and I might discover it, but that's alright. I think I know what it is. My father will pay me well for the information I will bring him. I saw it with my own eyes. You are a fast healer, like your father and grandfather."

"Wait, you lied to me." Magnus was shocked and backed away from the girl, "I thought you were here to entertain me?"

"I did, enough to distract you. In order to find your secret." Magnus's heart was racing, he was trying to find a way to make her forget and leave, and then he had an idea. "What did you like best, the love or the investigating?"

"Why do you ask?"

"Because if you like the love, I am willing to give you one last sign of my affection for you."

"Fine, a kiss for the road," the lady said and then kissed him with passion and treachery. Magnus was prepared and kissed back while directing her towards the bedside table. After a few rolls around the bed, Magnus pushed her over the edge, and she hit her head. Her evil smile turned straight as she mouthed, "How could you?"

As she fell into unconsciousness, Magnus replied, "Easy, I loved you, you betrayed me, and my secret must not be told," Then he shouted, "Help, this maiden fell and hit her head!" Innkeepers arrived and said, "That's the Leader's daughter. You better not tell him of this, lie and say you were out of the room."

"She is hardly dressed; we must tell her that she was asleep while you were out training and rolled out of bed."

Magnus did not disapprove and walked away to get ready for training. After four days of physical workout, he went back to focusing his mind. After four more fights, he was granted freedom, and the Leader's daughter looked at him with no memory of the four nights of romance. The Leader's nephew said as he gave the money, "Hope this helps your sister and your son, and whatever happened between my cousin and you will never be known for both my Uncle and I, know she was sent to spy, but after the accident, she has no memory."

"Sorry to hear that, but the money is now for my son. My sister was killed by a horse when she went out for a walk. She didn't hear it coming."

"Sorry for your loss hope to see your son here when I am Leader!"

"Maybe in twenty years' time!"

Magnus left and carved a stone to say "Sister and Aunty Mary" and then waited twenty years. During those twenty years, Alfred the Great of Wessex and his brother Aethelred fought many battles against the Danes during a Danish invasion and became King the next year, decided to construct a government and education system. Five years after that, the Danes invaded again, and for two years, King Alfred was forced to retire to the stronghold of Athelney, which was at that time an island in the Somerset Levels. The Russian nation was founded by Vikings under Prince Rurik, establishing the capital at Novgorod. A few years before becoming Maximus the second, a great victory at Edington in the year eight hundred seventy-eight by King Alfred secured the survival of Wessex. This was good news for Michel, for his heart was in the Kingdom. Michel returned to fight every twenty years, so the next time he fought under Marcus the second, King Alfred passed away, King Edward the Elder was crowned king, and he was only thirty. This carried on Michel winning money under a son of the previous Gladius. During the next wait in the year nine hundred and ten, the Benedictine monastery of Cluny in Burgundy becomes a place of monastic reform. The two major innovations here are the direct subjection of monasteries to the pope -- avoiding secular, local and ecclesiastical powers -- and the building of 'daughter monasteries' subordinate to the Cluniac family. And after four years of hiding after being under the name Magnus the second, King Edward died, and King Athelstan succeeded after him, son of the King's first wife Ecgwynn, at the age of thirty. But he died by the time Maximus, the third, went into the arena and was succeeded by his half-brother King Edmund, son of King Edward's third wife Edgiva, at eighteen. Four years after Otto the Great was crowned king in Germany, he succeeded in regaining control of Mercia.

After his father broke his grandfather's truce between Northumbrian and East Angles by attacking the South West of the Island, making the Danes attacked, taking over East Anglia in retaliation after fighting reciprocally. During the twenty years after winning his money, Marcus the third hears about Edmund's re-establishing control over Northumbria and ruling the united Anglo-Saxon Kingdom and expanding his rule into southern Scotland, only to be murdered three years later at the age of twenty-four at a party in Pucklechurch. His brother King Edred took over at twenty-three and ruled for nine years. Due to his illness, he died from bad health and was succeeded by his brother's first son King Edwy on January twenty-six at the age of fifteen, the same year John XII became pope at the age of eighteen. He caused a rebellion consisting of Mercians and Northumbrians, and he died a year before Marcus the third went into the arena.

Michel had fought families of other champions, and after one hundred years, he looked up to the throne. He sees the grandson of the first's leader sitting on the throne and his son, around twenty-five, sitting beside him and a girl aged in her twenties sitting next to him. She looked like the second leader's daughter and realised it was her great-granddaughter of his lover. She was wearing the same necklace, but another bead was added, and she was wearing black and realised that while her eldest cousin was Leader, he had no father, and his son had no brother. Marcus the third turned to see his opponent was great, great-grandson of the one he did not kill even with his illness. The man shouted, "My father spoke of the Gladius's, but he told me never to fight against one, but you look just like the coward that knocks himself out to draw a fight. I won't do the same!" and the fight ended with a club to the stomach. After five more fights, the winter came, and Marcus the third walked away with his money and went to become his son. When he arrived home, he heard a voice behind him "So this is where the infamous Gladius family lives, in a hut on the hill with a ring of tombstones."

Michel turned around to see that it was the girl who sat beside the throne. Michel stepped back towards the door and asked: "What brings you here, a mission for your Cousin, the Leader?"

"No, my mother was told by her father, who was told by her mother on her death bed, that your ancestor Magnus the first loved her and that your family had a secret. I only grew up around the arena to wait for your family's return and see them in battle. When I was eight months old, your father fought like a champion with the club that has been passed for generations."

"Well, now you have seen the house of my ancestors. What is keeping you here?" Michel's heart was racing as she stepped towards him and said, "You have the same eye colour, is that passed down for my great-grandmother remembered your face, with every detail the night she died a week before his son came into the arena. But you look like an exact copy, with no helmet to hide your face." She pushed him to the door and said: "Can I come in, or am I to assume your heir is inside with his mother?"

"My heir is out at the moment, and his mother died a week before I finished the fights."

"How convenient, you are alone at the moment!" She pushed him into the house and attacked his clothes with her nails. Helpless, Michel was seduced by his own lover's descendent. After a long night, he woke up to find her sitting on the floor, looking around the empty house and said, "You are alone, your son did not return, and there are no clothes fit for a woman in this house at all or even for a young boy. How come you lied to the innkeepers when you said you have a son?"

"I lied to protect a family secret, and now that you have come across it, I am conflicted between love for your family and my honour."

"What do you mean by love for my family? You only met my side of the family this year?"

"The truth would scare you, so I suggest you leave and keep this secret to yourself."

"I will leave as for this secret; I haven't got the slightest idea what it is, but I know I will never forget that if your heir comes, he isn't yours but one you adopted!"

She left, and for the next two seasons, Michel was conflicted. He walked around the house, looking at the box. He tipped it on the bed six months after the fight with the great-granddaughter. When a weak voice spoke from the doorway, "I have worked it out. You loved her, didn't you? I couldn't see it until I remembered your necklace, it has a bead like mine, and each bead represents a generation. My great grandmother mentioned she lost one of the beads to her necklace, so it would be a tradition to start a new and add a bead with the heir's coming." Michel turned around to see the twenty--year-old, standing short, with earth brown hair twice as long and nails twice as sharp. Her clothes were baggy, and she did not look like an heir to the throne of the arena. However, that wasn't what caught Michel's attention;

it was her body. She was larger than she was two seasons ago, it was the morning of San Juan (the twenty-fourth of June), and she was looking chubbier. She walked in and said, "You are Magnus which means you are your own son just so you cannot be killed for witchcraft."

"Who are you, and what makes you come into this house?" The confused Michel blurted out.

"My name is June, daughter of Julie and next to the throne of the arena if my cousin Septimus doesn't make it. I fell in love with a man, a stranger from a story of my great-grandmother, the daughter of the throne a century ago, who was named June as well. I am her exact split image, just like you were pretending to be his exact split image of your ancestor. I am the young woman that broke into your house, seduced you against your will and bore your child." To that, Michel fainted. For the next few seasons, June explained how she pretended to be a member of the town and found out she was with child. On the twenty-sixth of September, a baby boy was born into the house. He had the face and hair of his mother and the eyes of Michel. "Augustus, for he was born around the eighth month," June said and gave the baby a wash. For the next fifteen years, a lot happened both inside the house and outside the country. Mieczyslaw the first became the first ruler of Poland; Otto was named emperor in

Rome after defeating the Hungarians by Pope John XII. This meant that June was now under his rule, and her cousin, the leader of the games, had to give him money to continue the fights, which meant they lowered the prize money, and the penalty for loss was servitude to the new emperor. Winners get a third of the entry fee. Westminster Abbey was founded under the rule of King Edgar, King of all England, who died at the age of forty-five. Their son, who was now fifteen and his lover, who was the same age as him (physically not really), lived in their house.

Michel spoke on the night of Christmas in the year nine hundred and seventy-nine when Aethelred was King of England for his half-brother and Uncle died or were murdered. The Danes were attacking Chester and Southampton. "I cannot fight again, I cannot put people into servitude for the emperor, my family name may be a citizen, but I am truly a Frenchmen with a heart for England, and right now, they are in crisis."

"How can you leave? You have no money, no way to cross the seas and no chance that you will see your son again."

"Fine, I will fight for the money, but who can I pretend to be? I am meant to be fifty-five years old and still look thirty, and if I stay here, those tombstones will bear real names of people I love."

"Trust your heart, I am going to see if my cousin, for I am told is still in mourning of my disappearance and loss of his father, will accept the fact that I have an eighteen-year-old son from a stranger after a night of heartbreak and drinking. Do not think of him as your son, but as my son, and I am not your partner but your lover. I will leave; you will come in the New Year when the celebration of Easter has ended, for we are both children of faith." She left on the eve of the New Year, and when Magnus the third arrived to fight and had a quick look at his lover beside the throne with an heirless leader and her son beside him looking down. He received the necklace, and it had the bead that once belonged to his own great, great-grandmother. For the next hundred years, Michel used the money to build a ship while his home in England was being attacked. Even after Aethelred made a truce with Duke Richard I of Normandy, the Danes besieged London, which was bought off by Aethelred, Danes attacked Kent, and King Canute II of Denmark & Norway again invaded England. It was after the reigns of King Cnut, King Harold the first and King Edward the Confessor; the boat was finally ready and with one last look at his hut, which bears a tombstone that has two names "June, lady of beauty and her son Augustus, man of stamina." Michel went to the Arena for the last time as Magnus the fourth and called out, "Can I speak to the last heir of the June from Sicily?"

"Sicily was invaded by Normans, and Italy was created. Her family line grew larger in Italy, with her son having many children and them having many children. Still, only the eldest of the eldest is the heir, whom may I be speaking to, after eighty years of not hearing our great, great, great grandmother's name."

"My name is Magnus the fourth. I am a descendent of your Great, great grandmother's only true love. I am here to see her heir who wears the necklace."

"That would be me; my name is Primus Tempus, first son of the first son of the first son of Augustus."

"Can you come out?"

A boy aged twenty-one walked out wearing the necklace, then he looked down and said, "My great grandfather was right, you have every gene of your father's side, you look exactly like the painting which was based on a sketch Augustus did one day during a fight, it was titled 'Gladius the Gladiator'."

"Can I see it?"

"Better you can keep it, for I was told your family will be setting sail for England, and I hear that King Edward the Confessor is ruling England at this present time. Take the painting in memory of your ancestors, for there are plenty of paintings Augustus did of you."

"Thank you", Michel caught the dropped painting and walked to the shore with his boat and set sail to England.

Black Roses of Death

After eight days and twenty hours at sea, leaving on the first of January, Michel arrived on the ninth after passing Spain. He found out that Edward had died on his arrival, and now Harold was appointed the throne. Arriving at his house, which has miraculously survived the two hundred years of being unattended, Michel placed the painting on the wall and prayed. He wrote a letter to Primus the next morning and sent it over the border using a carrier pigeon. A fortnight later, he got his response.

"My grandfather is seventy-five, and my father is fifty-one. My youngest great Uncle moved to Milan and has two children, each with a family of their own. The son of Julius has twins, both ten years old. I have other great uncles and aunties, and they have kids; I know you were a family friend, but why do you ask such stupid questions? Of course, since Augustus, our family has grown. Our family is no longer in the business of Gladiators; we are in living in Italy from Sicily all the way to Milan. Hope the painting survived. We were each given something to remember him by -well, our grandfather's brother and sisters were. Julius was only given a notebook with the sketches and a secret message. My guess is it will take decades to discover. They each received something when they turned fifty."

Michel placed the letter in the box and smiled. His blood was throughout Italy. The next months passed, and soon it was June and Michel went into town. The baker called out, "Haven't seen that face for a while. Are you a Gelan? There are posters of you from centuries back."

"My name is Michael Gelan. Why do you ask?" Michel asked, worried someone knew about his secret.

"Just because there is a pile of letters from a friend of your family piled up at my house."

"Well, my family has been sailing trying to find a legendary fish. I guess I lost track of where and when, having been living on an island since birth. Thanks, I will collect them now."

Michel collected his own letters and used them for burning to keep himself warm during the night. It was soon September, and Harold the second struggled with the throne. It was not until the twentieth of September when Tostig and the Norwegian King Harald Hardrada came and battled English Soldiers. Michael was selected to fight, and he was lucky to avoid the onslaught with Harald and Tostig's men in the Battle of Fulford in York. A few days later, Michael found out that Tostig was Harold's banished brother, and on the twenty-fifth, Harold's men at Stamford Bridge defeated them. Michael fought the Norwegians and survived their weapons; his fighting style was strange, and one of the Norwegians shouted: "You fight like a Roman" as he picked up a branch and swung it at the horse.

"I was trained by the best!" Michael replied as the soldier flew forward and died by his own sword. The battle ended, and it was soon October. And Harold was still recovering; Michael was healed and was helping the wounded, but it was pointless, for their wounds were too deep, and the damage was too severe. He saw a woman on a hill writing on some paper during those days. After ten days, William's army in Pevensey attacked, infantry and England's surviving archers were outmatched, and Michael heard Harold's scream as he died. William had won and, on Christmas, was crowned King.

A year after the battle of Hastings, Michael wrote a letter to Primus telling him about the war and asked if they were managing, and it was not until October there was a reply. "Construction on the cathedral in Pisa, and some of my family are helping with the construction. We haven't heard from Julius's family since they left for Milan with the twins. I still cannot understand why a friend of Magnus would want to know, but we live even though there is a separation between the Eastern (Orthodox) and Western (Roman) churches. Primus."

The letters went back and forth for a few decades until a letter came in the year one thousand ninety-five from not Primus but his son.

"My father is fifty, and I am nineteen. My great grandfather passed away at the age of one hundred and four. My father has not heard from his family and only saw them at the funeral. Julius was not there, but his son, who is sixty-four, said that he is nearly one hundred and has given him the notebook and the code has not been cracked, they are happy in Milan, and his kids, the twins are nearly forty and in ten years will be getting the notebook, the youngest one that is. The eldest is married, and the youngest is dating a lady from Pisa."

A year after that letter, Michael was appointed for the first Crusade; he joined the knights and peasants to regain the Holy Land. As Michael the second, Michael marched with the Roman Catholics for days towards Constantinople, where they arrived there after a year of walking and setting up camps. They then moved on towards Antioch, where they arrived a year later. The terrain was harsh, and Michael hid his healing powers, but some of his fellow troops did not make it back alive. They arrived in the year one thousand and ninety-nine. Many people were lost from June seven to July fifteenth, and thousands of civilians were slaughtered.

Michael survived and returned home a few years later and wrote a letter to his family.

After decades of sending letters and signing them, Michael the third and fourth (friend of Magnus the fourth {died during the battle of the Hastings}), Michael was soon feeling the burden of his curse again. It was soon the year one thousand one hundred and forty-five. He prayed that if he was meant to do some good, please show him a sign, and when he was given a letter for recruitment for the second crusade, Michael gathered his club and sword and joined the legion. They arrived by boat in Lisbon in June, and on July first, they helped the Portuguese reclaim their land until October twenty-fifth, only to find out that their other half was attacked and killed on land, to Jerusalem. A few months later, they arrived in Jerusalem and participated in an ill-advised attack on Damascus. They returned home a loss, and forty-four years later, Michael the fifth was recruited for the third crusade under the orders of King John. This was also a failure after Emperor Frederick Barbarossa drowned in a river in Asia Minor on June 10th, a year after they left Europe. After driving the Muslims from Acre, Frederick's successor Leopold the fifth of Austria, and Philip left the Holy Land in August ninety-one. Saladin failed to defeat Richard in any military engagements, and Richard secured several more key coastal cities.

Nevertheless, on September second, ninety-two, Richard finalised a treaty with Saladin. Jerusalem would remain under Muslim control, allowing unarmed Christian pilgrims and merchants to visit the city. So they left, and after a month of walking, they sailed to England.

Six years later, Michael declined the call to participate in the fourth crusade and, after finding out what they did two years later, how they destroyed the library and robbed them of what they had. He was glad not to be part of it. Michael headed into London looking for a job to earn money and returned home after working with a blacksmith each night. He worked for that business for one hundred years under the sixth, seventh and eighth Michael. During this time, Genghis Khan invaded China, captured Peking, conquered Persia and invaded Russia. There was the Children's Crusade, the Fifth, Sixth, Seventh and Eighth Crusade. All that Michael declined after receiving notifications from King Henry the third. Marco Polo of Venice travelled to China, joined the Court of Kublai Khan, and returned to Genoa three years later after staying there for seventeen years. During that time, Khan governed China, became ruler of Mongols, established the Yuan dynasty in

China and invaded Burma. It wasn't until the year twelve
ninety-five when King Edward the first summons the Model
Parliament, which consisted of clergy and the aristocracy and
representatives from the various counties and boroughs.
Each county returned two knights, and two burgesses were
elected from each borough, and even each city provided two
citizens when Michael decided to leave London and travel
around England. He began in Hastings and headed west to
see how long it would take to return home. Walking at a slow
and steady pace watching as people live their lives, Michel
created a legend of a family of walkers. Every week, the man
is seen sitting, hardly eating, eyes closed on a rock. Beside
him were two sticks to tell the time and direction. This went
on for fifty years. Every winter, the man would rest until
winter was over and then walk again. The man would vanish
for eleven or twelve years, and suddenly, his son would walk
the edge of the United Kingdom. Michel was tired when he
reached the north and looked up to a hill and saw the same
woman standing there, watching him from a distance. Michel
thanked the Lord for the Angel as a sign of endurance,
prayed, and sang as he walked the earth.

"The Lord is my Shepherd; no want shall I know. I feed in
green pastures; safe-folded I rest. He leadeth my soul where
the still waters flow, restores me when wand'ring, redeems

when oppressed, restores me when wand'ring, redeems
when oppressed. Thru the valley and shadow of death
though I stray, since thou art my Guardian, no evil I fear. Thy
rod shall defend me, thy staff be my stay. No harm can befall
with my Comforter near. No harm can befall with my
Comforter near. In the midst of affliction, my table is spread.
With blessings unmeasured my cup runneth o'er. With
perfume and oil, thou anointest my head. Oh, what shall I ask
of thy providence more? Oh, what shall I ask of thy
providence more?" which was his song for the Bible verse,
"The Lord is my shepherd, I lack nothing. He makes me lie
down in green pastures, he leads me beside quiet waters,
and he refreshes my soul. He guides me along the right paths
for his name's sake. Even though I walk through the darkest
valley. I will fear no evil, for you are with me; your rod and
your staff, they comfort me. You prepare a table before me
in the presence of my enemies. You anoint my head with oil;
my cup overflows. Surely your goodness and love will follow
me all the days of my life, and I will dwell in the house of the
Lord forever."

Michel arrived home on Wednesday the ninth of
August thirteen forty-six and spent the next few months
getting his old alias ready for a new year as a Matthew Gelan
descendant of the famous Gelan. Heading into the heart of

London in November, a few months later, Matthew sends a letter to his family saying he is a descendant trying to find the owner of the necklace. As Matthew watched the pigeon fly away, he turned just in time to see a boy trying to pick up money scattered around his feet. Matthew went over to help pick them up and asked: "Why in a hurry?"

"My Mother needs food. I must get something for her to eat."

Matthew saw a market, bought some bread and meat, and asked, "Where is your mother? I will take this to her?"

Matthew followed the boy to a side street where his mother was sitting, her eyes were empty, and Matthew could tell she was blind. "Mother, I have brought food. This kind man gave me some bread and meat."

"Listen, if you want a house, I have a home In Hastings available."

"Mum, rather be here to listen to the street gossip." The boy replied and held out his hand, "My name is Walter."

"Well, Walter, I am Matthew Gelan."

"Gelan as in…."

"The Gelan family was in England since the year four hundred, so yes, Gelan as in whatever you were about to say."

Walter smiled, and when Matthew left, he went home feeling sorry for the boy. End of October, a pigeon returned with a letter.

"I am the wearer of the necklace, my name is Belinda, my ancestor Primus passed it on to his first child, and it was given to hers and then given to his and then to me. We live in Sicily, and our family is spread across the whole of Rome. Julius's family still lives in Milan, and we have family members working in Pisa after their ancestors help build the Pisa buildings since ten sixty-eight. They are still mending the tower of Pisa, which is leaning. Even after a hundred years of waiting, the architects still made errors to cause the lean. If you wish, you can continue to communicate, and as for the secret message in the notebook, I have not heard a word about it, but that is from my cousins from Julius's side, who are secretive and protective."

After a year of sending letters and a pigeon arrived from Italy, the letter was marked urgent. "Matthew, I write bearing bad news, some strange disease has arrived on our shores, dozens of people are ill, and hundreds have died. I have lost Uncles, Aunts and cousins. I am fleeing to Venice to get away. Warn your people to not let anyone enter their shores."

Matthew ran to the shores to spread the word, but they laughed at the idea and called him crazy. He rushed to London and, after a week, arrived and tried to warn the people. Everyone laughed. After a few attempts, Matthew decided to leave, and then he heard a boy scream in pain. Rushing over to the location of the scream, Matthew arrived to find Walter holding a leg, which was gushing with blood. Matthew saw a metal pipe and a branch. Giving the branch to Walter, he said, "Bite this," and without thinking twice, he pierced his arm with the metal pipe and watched as the blood flowed into the open wound. He then saw a hot iron for horseshoes and used it to burn the flesh. Picking the boy up, he carried him to the street where his mother was and saw her sitting waiting for her son to arrive. Matthew covered his wound with his sleeve and used the leg of the pants to cover Walter's. "Listen, we have to get you both to my house. Walter is injured, and you are blind." A week later and they arrived at the house. For the next two months, Matthew cared for Walter as his leg healed within a couple of days, and Matthew's was already scar-free. Walter's mum became attached to Matthew, and on the first of January, they got married by a pastor and returned home to find a pigeon waiting. Matthew opened the letter and read aloud, "The Plague arrived in Venice. I am moving to Pisa with my surviving relatives. I have already lost half my family. I don't know about Julius, will keep in touch, Belinda."

After another two weeks of watching Walter and Paris (Walter's mother) adjust to their new life, Matthew received another pigeon. This letter was written in red ink and said, "The Plague reached Pisa, and I think I won't make it past another month. I do not think I can get my necklace to you. I have already decided to burn our house on my death. My family is dead, my father, mother and brother, my cousins from Pisa to Sicily are dead, I have some from further north and others who are out at sea. I hope they make it. My necklace will be given to you on my death."

Matthew lived with his wife for the next few months, and on the twentieth of May, Matthew received a letter from a pigeon, but it was burnt, and the bird was injured. The letter said, "Matthew, the necklace is with the bird, I have burned my house, I told the bird to fly once there was smoke, everything that was in our home was burnt, the paintings are gone, and they would have been in danger of spreading the bug to you if they arrived. The family secret of ours would die if the line of Julius was to die by the plague, but I will die knowing there was a friend of the family caring for us...... Be"
the rest was burnt; Matthew looked and saw no necklace. Unknown to him, a young girl aged twenty arrived with a

mask and went to collect the paintings and saw the necklace in the rubble. This was while the fire burned. The girl left and was never seen again. Matthew's warning became true when a ship arrived in June, and the plague spread from France up to Portugal and even down to Spain. London was affected, and soon everyone was crying out with regret for not believing Matthew. For the next few years, Matthew told Walter (who was ten) to stay indoors and only he went out to find food. He fished for fresh fish and found his own vegetables. The Plague didn't affect him, and by the time the plague reached Russia in fifty-one, Walter was thirteen and was ready to explore. With the blood of Matthew flowing through his veins, he was immune to the Black Plague, which was the name given to the plague that wiped out thirty to sixty per cent of the population. Matthew let him get food and warned him to keep to the main streets. Matthew wrote a letter and hoped it would return, but it did not. Matthew guessed that no one lived in the area. He prayed that his family under the line of Julius was not affected. A few years later, when Walter was sixteen, Matthew was ordered to serve in the war against France. Matthew told Walter to look after his mother. He left and went into battle; the year was thirteen fifty-four, and Walter smiled as his father left for battle.

Two years later, Matthew helped capture King James the Second. They knighted him and gave him a shield with a bear, dove, and club. Matthew continued in the war even past the point when the Black Prince was made Duke. Only when John Chandos was killed did Matthew leave. He arrived to find his son, now thirty-two, looking after his old mother. Walter turned and said, "Dad, you have not aged one bit. How come?"

"Son, there is something I must tell you, and you must promise to keep it between you and me. I can only die if I cannot recover from an attack. This means drowning, a stab to the heart which I cannot pull out and a broken neck from a hanging."

"So, you survived the war because of this, and then what made you come home?"

"Your mother is not like me. I came back so she could spend her last few years with her husband."

That is exactly what Matthew did for the next four years when his son turned thirty-six and found a woman to love. The three watched the last minutes of Paris fade from her face. She smiled and said, "Matthew, I was lucky to find a man to raise my boy and a man that loved me with all his heart."

After she was buried, Matthew watched Walter leave to marry his true love, and before he did, he said, "Listen, I am going overseas. This will be the last time I will see you, you know my secret. I must change names, and to do this, I must die. You will understand when the letter arrives." Matthew sailed down to France and, as he did, sent a pigeon back with word of 'his drowning.' He arrived on French soil, and being the year thirteen seventy-six, he found out that The Black Prince was dead and in the middle of the battle. He took sail, headed north, and arrived in the Country of Iceland. He arrived a year later when King Richard the second became King.

Matthew watched the world battle around him for the next eighty years, sitting in a cave on the coast, never changing. The pigeons to his stepson's family were the only source of information; he found out that King Richard died in the year fourteen hundred after being imprisoned in Pontefract Castle and The Canterbury Tales disappeared after the death of the writer. Henry the fourth took the throne and English. That Henry the fifth was crowned king on April nine, fourteen thirteen and died at the age of thirty-five after marrying King Charles the sixth's daughter Catherine of Valois in fourteen twenty. So that the King would be of both territories, who was named king less than a year old, but

Charles the seventh disapproved and continued battle. When the king is two, he heard that his regent, Humphrey, Duke of Gloucester, marries Jacqueline, Countess of Hainaut, and invades Holland to regain her former dominions, bringing him direct conflict with Philip III, Duke of Burgundy. At the age of eighteen, a female breaks a siege and then is sold to England to be executed by fire for being a witch a year later. That year (fourteen thirty-one), Matthew looks at his box of letters and tokens and decides to bury it along with the memories they carry. His hair has grown long, and he had a beard, for he did not shave. He used his undershirt to mark where it was located, using the stars and seas to guide him. He then sent a letter to his family to get a response from Petunia, aged eleven, and her brothers Petro and Michael (after his step-great grandfather's real name), saying Henry the sixth of England was crowned King of France in Paris. Charles was King as well. He found out that twenty-two years later, Petro, now aged forty, was married, and with a son named Warren, the King was mentally ill, and the war was finished.

Putting Art into our Hearts- Dawn of the Renaissance

Michel sent no more letters and set sail to Italy ten years later to see if his other family survived the Plague. He arrived a year later to find the place was still recovering from the Plague, the plague was still around, but it was isolated. It has been over one hundred years since the plague and been around one hundred years since he got no response. He walked to the household he sent the pigeon to, only to find it in ruins. Being the year fourteen sixty-three, the whole of Italy was changing. They were becoming happy and artistic to forget the pain of the plague, but when Michel walked inside the burnt house and saw everything as dust, he was overcome with sorrow. Then he saw the beds and then went outside through a hole to see a slab of stone with a list of names of everyone that died that belonged to this house. Michel became sad and walked around Italy to see how much had changed.

He noticed that when he arrived in ten days, the Doors of the Cathedral were done by Andrea Pisano and the north and east doors by Lorenzo Ghiberti. He saw people painting in their homes. He caught the names of a few, some being Andrea Mantegna, Piero Della Francesca (when he arrived in Sansepolcro) and Dieric Bouts. He heard music being played in the streets and saw sculptures being made. Michel decided to start off new and went to some workshops. He changed his name to Mitchell.

Mitchell Green learned the arts, but he found out that; Charles the Bold succeeded as Duke of Burgundy and Ivan the Great rules Russia, so Mitchell decided to create a sculpture called "The Greats in history." He had the help of the winner of the Gates to Paradise, Lorenzo, until he became ruler of Florence a year or so later. Mitchell Green went to Donatello and continued his artwork of the Greats in history. It so far consisted of Jesus, David, King Alfred, Ivan and a few other leaders. Donatello was impressed by the accuracy of some of their faces and was pleased to see Jesus and David at the top. (They made a 'great' pyramid of the people). As Mitchell learnt the arts, the events in England changed around him. First, while Edward is King, Warwick falls out with him and defeats him at Edgecote. They are later reconciled, but Warwick is banished. He makes peace with Margaret, returns to England with an army, and Edward flees to Flanders. To this, Henry is remade, King. Men were recruited for the war because the House of York did not like Henry in charge; Michel declined and continued learning the ropes. One year later, when Edward returns to England from

Flanders and defeats and kills Warwick at the Battle of Barnet, Margaret, King Henry's wife, is defeated at the Battle of Tewkesbury, does the Lancastrian heir, Prince Edward, gets killed. Soon after, Henry the sixth is murdered in the Tower of London. Mitchell continues to paint, create music and sculpt under the watchful eyes of the heroes when he gets to have a peek at the Morte d'Arthur, which Sir Thomas Malory completed a few years ago.

During the time of creativity, rumours have spread of a girl with sunshine gold hair or her daughter reappearing with a scroll writing what she sees. Sometimes, Mitchell spots her on the hillside a few times and wonders if she was an angel or another immortal. He painted a picture of her and placed it in his cloth bag. The first printing press was created by William Caxton in Westminster, London, which led to new ideas such as the clocks without weights but with springs and coils. Edward falls out with his brother George, Duke of Clarence, who is then murdered in the Tower, supposedly in a butt of malmsey wine. With the death of the composer Guillaume Dufay, Mitchell wrote a song called 'endless melodie', which went like this

"From the beginning of man, music filled the world, from the bird calls to the cries of a girl. Music that filled the hearts of the people to spread peace, warnings and entertainment will never cease. Trumpets can end, drums can go silent, flutes and fifes can break, but the melody will never end.

Songs of the ages, an endless melodie, songs of the ages will play forever and always. The minstrels and jongleurs play for the entertainment of the court, but the Kings can stop that with one word. The sound of horns in battle and the drums to spread the truth can be stopped with a weapon of man, but the melodies will never end. Song of the ages and endless melodies, songs of the ages will play forever and always"

Years went by, and after hearing word of a prodigy had been born named Michelangelo around this time, Hugo van der Goes of Ghent, a famous painter, died, and Richard the third became King of England. Richard only lasted two years, and then King Henry the seventh became King. Mitchell travelled around Italy and saw many new creations, and soon he needed to change. He left saying he had a family to go to, and a year later, Michael Green came and began his tours.

Michael spotted thirteen-year-old Michelangelo, and with the War of Roses ended, Michael decided to paint his perspective of the world. He found the colours he wanted and started to oil paint. First, he painted a sphere, blue and white. After that, he painted Europe filling the whole sphere almost. That took a few days. After a rest, he began again.

First, he painted a man. He made sure it did not look like him, he then painted smaller people around the whole of the page, and their colours weren't all white. Michael painted some yellow, some red, and some black and then showed it to his mentor, then Leonardo, who came down from Milan after being told by Donatello about his work. He smiled and muttered, "you have quite the imagination, people black and yellow, but we haven't crossed the seas to find out, so you might be right."

After that, Michael got to work on his next project. He needed wood, metal (bronze and gold), paint, and clay. The first thing he did was carve four sixteen-inch by sixteen-inch pieces of wood with grooves that made pits and peaks on all of them in one-two patterns. He then painted the wood green and brown, the grooves brown and the peaks green. That took Michael three days. After that, Michael rushed over to the library to get some research. He looked around and saw the blonde woman holding a book and putting it back. She walked out the door. Michael went over to the section of the library to see a book (one of the first delivered from England) labelled "Family that travelled the country" Michael opened the book and began to read,

"In the year fourteen forty-two, a man was seen walking from Hastings upwards. He followed the shoreline in rain or shine. He walked on. After a week, the man stopped and sat on a rock, placed sticks beside him and then closed his eyes and started to mutter. After ten days a boy went up to hear what the traveller was saying and came back repeating these words 'The Lord is my shepherd, I lack nothing. He makes me lie down in green pastures, he leads me beside quiet waters, and he refreshes my soul. He guides me along the right paths for his name's sake' Thirty days later, the eyes opened, and the man walked on. This time he was spotted further north of Portsmouth in Southampton two days later. From there, the man walked up to Abbotsbury and rested again for forty days, not eating, only drinking. From there, the man walked for another seven days arriving around Plymouth. After the forty days of rest, the man continued to walk for seven days to Wadebridge." Michael stopped and saw the sketch of his face before the long hair realised that people had spotted him through his walk. "Ilfracombe was near where he rested for the fifth time, and today was the seventeenth of September. He arrived at waters near Bristol after six weeks of walking and five lots of forty days' rest. The man wasn't stopping, he vanished for eleven years, and a man continued, around Bristol, Cardiff, Haverfordwest….."

Michael put the book down and saw another two books labelled "Family of the Sword, the Line of Gladius" and "The unscathed Knight", and he finally found what he wanted to find and rushed over to continue his masterpiece. Michael was hand carving and moulding out of the bronze, gold, and clay for the next few weeks. He made castles from bronze, horses from clay, people from bronze and men from clay. He finally made a few kings and queens and allowed them to dry. He went back to the library and found the book; he read a section from the Family of the Sword.

"Maximus Gladius was a foolish fighter. He went into battle without any armour. He was thrown the minute he closed his eyes. But he stood up and tossed stones into the face of his opponent. The stones startled him while the net tripped him, making him the winner, then he chose to let the man live and fought alongside the champion after that. Together they beat the reigning champion hacking his ankle and hitting him in the jaw. Gladius then held a sword and a club. After he won, his son came... Marcus" Michael skipped a few and read on, "Magnus was up against the champion's heir, and they fought like mad. Magnus began by charging with the weapon that once belonged to their family. Atticus, the grandson, dodged and kicked Magnus in the back and into a wall. Magnus pushed off the wall and jumped onto the wall, and started to walk along the edge. When Magnus got out of range, he picked up a rock and tossed it at Atticus's skull. Atticus used his sword to block the attack and then charged. Jumping over with legs apart, Magnus managed to land behind him and kick him in the back like a horse making Atticus fall over the wall. That made Atticus furious, and he picked up a huge piece of rock and tossed it at Magnus. Magnus jumped aside. Falling for the trap, Magnus waited for the right time and when Atticus charged sword high, ready to cut the shoulder blade. Meanwhile, Magnus was using the club as a cane, and when the shadow of Atticus was over his, Magnus raised the club and hit Atticus straight in the nose; the sword dropped, missing his feet by inches, and Atticus staggered; backwards in pain."

Michael returned to the workshop and began to paint the sculptures. First, he painted faces on the knights and bishops and then painted faces on the foot soldiers. Leonardo was looking impressed and confused at this piece of art but suddenly saw what it was and said, "Well, my boy, you created the pieces of Chess, but that looks like King Henry and Richard of York as the kings, and some of the kings look like famous kings from history."

"They are. These games represent four famous battles, the King and Queen here represent Margaret and Henry, Edward and Elizabeth."

"I see that is very clever. We will play a game to see how they fare when it dries. Let me guess the green and brown represent dirt and grass?"

"Yes, they do. It represents the battlefields."

"Very good indeed."

As promised, after they were dry the winter of eighty-eight, Leonard and Michael played a chess game. Leonardo, while playing, spoke of his famous designs. "I have painted since the fourteen seventy, and I have done; The Annunciation, the Baptism of Christ, Madonna of the Carnation, Ginevra de Benci, Benois Madonna, The Adoration of the Magi, St. Jerome in the Wilderness Portrait of a Musician", he paused and moved a piece and then continued after Michael moved out of check. "I am still working on Madonna Litta and Virgin of the Rocks, but I am having a break while looking at your work."

"What else have you done?" He asked as he lost a knight to the queen of King Henry.

"I have invented the flying machine so one day man can fly, I tried to make some from a few ideas a couple of years ago, and one of them was this spiral bladed flying-machine and a light hang-glider. Mostly they were useless and did not work, like my screw helicopter design for it that machine could not provide lift. However, my hang glider has been successfully constructed and demonstrated based on my designs. Others include pulleys and gears; these can help power the world!"

With that, Henry defeated Edward and Leonardo left for Milan. "Take me with you; I want to see if I can find someone."

"Are they a friend?"

"Maybe. It's been ages since I heard from them."

"Sure, I have two horses." With that, Michael left for Milan. They arrived a few days later, around December first. Walking around, Michael asked around for someone named Tempus (the surname his love took when they split Tempus, meaning time) and when he arrived at the house that belonged to a Bartholomew Tempus-Maximus. Knocking on the door, two kids around sixteen years old came to the door and asked: "Who is this?"

"My name is Michael Green; my family was friends with the Gelan I wonder if you know of Julius Tempus?"

"Dad, Pa, there is a man asking about Julius!"

A frail voice broke the air, and an elderly man stepped out and said, "Strange, I thought you were the man on the back of the notebook for a second."

"Notebook, what do you mean?" Michael asked, knowing about the notebook but not about the sketch.

"On the back of the book is a picture of the man that was Augustus's father and the first page has a message "Find my father's secret, it is written on his face.""

"I did not know of that. That wasn't told by Gelan."

"Son, can you bring the notebook? It will be yours someday next year!" minutes later a man arrived, he was holding a book trapped in glass. The grandfather opened the book and showed him the picture using a key. Michael stared into the face of Mitchell Gelan and of Magnus Gladius. Then he saw letters inside his face and said: "I see letters, such as O and X, maybe find all the letters and a message could be formed."

"That's a lead. We haven't had a lead in fifteen generations. Thank you, want to come in and have dinner."

Michael had dinner with their family, which changed to staying until the twins' twentieth birthday. During that time, Michael made them a present, a chessboard and pieces to represent the Roman and Greek gods, plus the pawns were Roman Legions and Greek Demigods. They were born on the first of January, and when Janus and Judas turned the age, Michael left and headed to Spain for a new life. He lied and said he would visit family and then left on a horse. Before he crossed the borders, he cut half the length of his hair to make it shorter, and then he shaved his beard and crossed into France, found new clothes in Lyon (still wearing his same undershirt), and walked for days into Spain. He arrived in Spain days later. He arrived in Madrid in June and stayed for a few months. He caught word about a sailor heading into the unmarked seas on the West and decided to join in. He left the inn under his new alias Micah Grain. He found the ship Santa María jumped aboard, and fell asleep.

Small Step into a Whole New World

Micah woke up and found himself with the gunpowder and supplies at the bottom of the ship. He didn't know how long he was asleep, then he heard talking above, "Twenty days at sea and we are already down to our last lot of supplies; luckily, the Canary Islands is a week away."

Micah calculated and realised he was in the middle of the sea, heading towards the Canary Islands. He hasn't eaten in twenty days and might be spotted in a week. Micah decided to stay hidden and hope they won't kill him on sight; otherwise, his secret would be out.

A week later and Micah heard someone coming down the stairs and after the barrels were taken, a voice spoke in Spanish with an Italian accent "Sé que estás aquí, que fueron vistos hace dos semanas. Que estaba dormida siento que fuiste a soñar."

"Sorry. No hago mucho español."

"Englishmen, you were spotted a fortnight ago. We left you to dream. What is your name?"

"Micah, Micah Grain."

"Well, Mr Grain, can you shoot a firearm and work on a ship?"

"Yes!"

"Then join us. We lost a man at sea."

"Thank you, listen, where are we exactly?"

"The Canary Islands, west of Spain and heading towards the Newfoundland or the unknown!"

"Ok, I only worked on a boat with my dad. I have never been out to sea this far before." Micah half lied; he has been at sea but never to an unknown location. The man introduced himself as Cristóbal Colón "...but you can call me Christopher."

Micah shook hands and then was led to the top of the boat and onto the shore. There they restocked and mended the ship. They then left on the sixth and headed west towards the unknown. On the ship, Micah helped with the ropes and sails and, after a nice breeze left him with nothing to do that night, called Christopher over for a chess game. He pulled out an ordinary chess set; Micah left the chess sets with Leonardo and said someone would ask for them. Christopher laughed and said in Spanish, "Usted es un hombre divertido." and then stopped and said, "I like you, you like a challenge, ok, one game of chess."

Micah was black, and Christopher was white, but they made a small bet before playing. "Whoever loses will have to listen to what the other person says. In other words, if I lose Micah,

I will listen to your story and not leave you on the next land we set sail on."

Using the skills Leonardo taught him, he ended up winning against Christopher. Christopher sighed and then smiled.

"Perdí, así que lo que usted dice voy a escuchar y obedecer." suddenly, from one of the other ships, the Pinta, Rodrigo de Triana, the lookout was jumping up and down, in which the captain of the Pinta, Martín Alonso Pinzón, verified the discovery and alerted Columbus by firing a Lombard. Christopher told his crew, including Micah, that he saw the light early that morning when they got back to shore, but Micah knew that was a lie, for he had been playing chess since midnight. They arrived on the island around five o'clock, and Christopher christened the island San Salvador. They began to explore the new land when they awoke many people. After a day of miscommunication, Micah and Christopher finally communicated, and it was the morning of the thirteen.

Micah kept close to Christopher and saw what he wrote in his notebook on the first night. "Saturday, 13 October 1492: ... They brought us sticks of the cotton thread and parrots and other little things which it would be tedious to list and exchanged everything for whatever we offered them. I kept my eyes open and tried to find out if there was any gold, and I saw that some of them had a little piece hanging from a hole in their nose. I gathered from their signs that if one goes south or around the island's south side, there is a king with great jars full of it enormous amounts. I tried to persuade them to go there, but I saw that the idea was not to their liking..." Micah realised that Christopher was keen to look for gold and read his previous day "Many of the men I have seen have scars on their bodies, and when I made signs to them to find out how this happened, they indicated that people from other nearby islands come to San Salvador to capture them; they defend themselves the best they can. I believe that people from the mainland come here to take them as slaves. They ought to make good and skilled servants, for they repeat very quickly whatever we say to them. I think they can very easily be made Christians, for they seem to have no religion. If it pleases our Lord, I will take six of them to Your Highnesses when I depart so that they may learn our language." Micah decided to explore during the night and, after a few hours, returned at sunrise and watched as one of Christopher's men sought a fight with an elder and won. A day of them fighting and trading, Micah watched as Christopher wrote in his notepad, and an idea formed when he read the last few sentences "Sunday, 14 October 1492: ... These people have little knowledge of fighting, as Your

Majesties will see from the seven I have had captured to take away with us so as to teach them our language and return them unless Your Majesties' orders are that they all be taken to Spain or held captive on the island itself, for with fifty men one could keep the whole population in subjection and make them do whatever one wanted."

That morning Micah was standing before the Arawak tribe and shouted to Columbus's men, "You will return those you have taken prisoner or fight me in singlestick combat; if I lose, you will be able to take them, and you can leave me here to die. If I win, you release them, and I will show you the gold I have discovered."

The men looked surprised, and Christopher shouted, "Hombre estúpido, es necio, hizo un reto que no puede ganar." Micah translated as "Stupid man is a fool, made a challenge he cannot win."

Micah shouted, "Guess that means you will take up the challenge of Canne de combat."

Christopher nodded and said, "Bring out the prisoners. They can watch this stowaway lose for their sake."

Micah saw the type of man that Christopher was and shouted, "You promised you would listen to what I have to say, so listen, I have travelled far and wide for something new, and I will not allow you to destroy this civilisation. You are a greedy man, so here's something to add to your greed, all my money will be yours if I lose, you can have it all, but if I win, you will only take a willing volunteer with you on your ship!"

"Fine with me!"

Micah held a stick out and, after drawing a circle about ten feet in diameter and said: "Let's begin." Christopher tried to strike at Micah, but he dodged it and struck Christopher on the shoulder. Christopher got furious and tried again to hit Micah, but Micah was quick and hit him repeatedly. The Arawak people were cheering, and Columbus's men were shocked at how he was fighting with such grace and anger. They watched as Christopher's fury built up, and his rage made him sloppy and then charged at Micah after an hour of misses. Micah stepped aside and said, "You know you lose once you take one foot outside the circle, right?"

"I will beat you, peasant. You are just a stowaway!" Christopher snapped and cursed in Spanish when he got hit in the shoulder.

"Watch your temper, you promised to listen to me, but I see that you are just a greedy, selfish sailor trying to please the Kings and Queens with tales of new land. Well, beat me, and the proof will be fifteen men. Lose, and the proof will be one man."

Christopher's face was red with frustration and tiredness when he charged again. Micah stepped aside and used the stick to tap him on the shoulder blades pushing Christopher over the circle.

"You let your anger take hold of you; you didn't register what I said!"

"And what was that, Micah Grain?"

"Even with one man, you will please their Majesties."

"Very well, now you said something about gold."

"Why yes, follow me," Micah led them to what was a river and said. "The only gold is small specks. Their gold was from their home island before they moved. We better leave with the youngest and the strongest, so he can survive the trip. Now listen to Christopher. We have a journey to take without you becoming all greedy and selfish."

"Spoken like a man that's seen it all before."

"In a past life, but we better go. The sun is setting, and we have to leave early tomorrow morning."

For the next fortnight, they travelled around the islands and towards the coast of Cuba. Christopher explored the coast, they arrived on the coast on the twenty-eighth, and from there, they sailed up the coast, porting every night.

Christopher was beginning to become less selfish but got annoyed that the Pinta vanished on November twenty-second, a month after exploring the coast of Cuba. After a few days, he didn't care and continued to sail towards the coast of what was to be called Hispaniola. They landed on the fifth and began to explore. Micah was in charge of the new passenger, and Micah taught him how to fight and defend himself. While the ship sailed beside the coast, "Christopher, Micah and the new passenger walked the shoreline. Micah had taught the man about the Bible, and he started to learn to read and write.

"You a man of faith, Micah?" Christopher asked after two weeks of walking.

"As long as I can remember, yes, I am," Micah replied.

"Explains why you are the better man", Christopher muttered as they turned back and headed back to the main area so they could sail further down. In the distance, Micah saw the girl sitting on a hill near where they first landed, he blinked, and she was gone.

"Why did you save the natives on the other island?"

"Call it a vision or a sign of goodwill," Micah replied.

Another week walking for Christopher and Micah, and their ship was coming in to pick them up, and the waves pushed it faster to shore. Suddenly the boat was on shore broken, and the other boat was still out at sea.

The people jumped onto the shore and shouted, "we can't all reach the other boat. There are not enough lifeboats."

The natives that Micah and Christopher encountered came and said: "Some are welcome here to stay."

Christopher opened his mouth and then closed it and turned to Micah. "What does your heart tell you?"

"Me, I believe that everyone can make it to the other boat if we build a raft and row back."

"Row, are you mad? The waves are pushing everything to shore."

"I am not mad; I am thinking what is best for the crew. I will build the raft. It's that or captain, you take turns picking up your crew."

"Build the raft; the seas aren't safe for another trip."

Two days later, a raft was built, and they all made it on the boat after two hours of rowing. They made it to the ship and set sail to the Peninsula he spotted on their walk. The ship arrived two weeks later and set anchor. Micah, Christopher and ten men walked the shore until they encountered the hostile Ciguayos, who presented him with his only violent resistance. They refused to trade. After one of Christopher's crew stabbed two for not trading arrows,

Micah stepped between and got shot with arrows in the chest. He pulled them out and said, "No more violence. These arrows will be another of a fair bargain. You can survive with six." And they left and headed back to Spain. But after a month of rough seas, they ended up getting pushed off course and landed in Lisbon. They finally arrived back in Spain with two new passengers on the fifteenth.

After a few months, Micah was asked to keep his men in line, and since they had twelve hundred people to settle, Christopher was asked to make sure the natives agreed to their stay. They left for the Canary Islands, and after repeating what they did on the first voyage, they departed on the thirteenth of October. They sailed south, and on the third of November, Columbus sighted a rugged island that he named Dominica. The next day, he landed on an island that Columbus named "'Santa María de Guadalupe de. Extremadura', after the image of the Virgin Mary." Christopher was pleased by the sight of some of the inhabitants. He noticed Micah asleep and decided to get one of his men (a friend from his childhood named Michele da Cuneo) to influence the women to join them for a few days. Micah explored with Christopher the island on the morning of the ninth and returned to hear a scream from aboard the ship; Micah ran on board and followed the scream. He opened the door to find a native woman wearing what her people wore and Christopher's best friend holding a rope. The native was covering signs of being whipped. Micah turned to Christopher, who muttered, "I wanted them on the ship as guides. I was planning to clothe them, I didn't...." But Micah could tell he was lying, and he went to punch Michele in the face, but Christopher hit him over the head, and Michele used the rope to tie him up. Micah woke up on the night of the ninth to hear above him the sounds of the floor and the crying of a lady. With his head feeling better, he got up, went to the source, pulled Michele off the indigenous woman, and punched him in the jaw. "Get all the others, now all I will show you how I defeated your friend Christopher on the island of Juana", Michele obeyed, and Micah turned to the scared and injured lady. "Listen, get off the boat tonight. We leave tomorrow morning, just go. I am sorry for what this man did to you."

They left the island and the men of the island shouted curses at Michele and Christopher. Micah blinked and saw a girl on a hill, and then when he blinked again, she was gone. They arrived in Haiti twelve days later, where they found the fort that Christopher set up last time in ruins and ashes and the two men that stayed behind dead. Christopher got angry and demanded to see everyone over the age of fourteen. Micah overheard what he was planning to do. When they arrived stood before the indigenous people and shouted, "Christopher, you cannot expect your people to go well with the others. I suggest you keep your punishments to yourself. If you want gold, find some and then go. If you want to hurt them, you must hurt me, but you have seen how I fight. You know I can win." They sailed east and found a new spot for the people to the land and colonize. They left a few months later after celebrating New Year's Day, Ash Wednesday, Palm Sunday, Good Friday and Easter Sunday. It was the twenty-fourth and after a few days on the water arrived a week later on the south coast of what Christopher named Juana (our day Cuba) and came to a conclusion as being a peninsula of Asia. After five days of not touching land, they arrived at an island where they rested for a night and then moved out, retracing their steps. They arrived back on Hispaniola on the twentieth of August. They returned to Spain, where Micah left for an inn, and Christopher told of his adventures, leaving out the part about getting caught breaking a commandment and nearly getting beaten by Micah. Micah trimmed his hair and got ready for another few years with Christopher.

Micah waited four years when he was called to the port; Christopher was finally leaving for his third voyage.

They left port on the thirtieth of May with three of the six ships. The other three went directly to Hispaniola. The other three ships with Micah had sailed to Christopher's first wife's island called Porto Santo. Christopher paid his respects and then turned to Micah and asked, "You married?"

"No," Micah lied, thinking about his first love and their son and then his first wife and her son. "Never really considered staying in one spot."

"Well, I have twice; my first wife lived here; shame she died." Then they sailed to Madeira and spent some time there with the Portuguese captain João Gonçalves da Camara before sailing to the Canary Islands and Cape Verde. Which was south of the Canary Islands. They had enough supplies to make them there, which meant they stopped to restock. They sailed west across the Atlantic Ocean when Columbus discovered that his compass and the stars didn't match up. Micah himself had a compass, and when they arrived on an island months later from leaving Spain. The ships landed on the southern coast of the island of Trinidad on the last day of July. From there, they stepped off and explored. The crew collected supplies, and they soon were back on the ship heading west along the coast. From the fourth to the twelve, Columbus explored the Gulf of Paria, which separates Trinidad from what is now Venezuela, near the delta of the

Orinoco River. From there, their ships touched dry land on the Paria Peninsula.

Columbus correctly interpreted the enormous quantity of freshwater that the Orinoco delivered into the Atlantic Ocean as evidence that he had reached a continental landmass during the next few days. As he sailed the Gulf of Paria, he observed the diurnal rotation of the pole star in the sky, which he erroneously interpreted as evidence that the Earth was not perfectly spherical. He then sailed to the islands of Chacachacare and Margarita. He sighted Tobago (which he named "Bella Forma") and Grenada (which he named "Concepción"). Columbus returned to Hispaniola on the nineteenth of August not feeling very well, only to find that many of the Spanish settlers of the new colony were in rebellion against his rule, claiming that Columbus had misled them about the supposedly bountiful riches of the New World. Christopher tried to calm them down and turned to Micah, who was walking away. He headed to La Isabela, and when Christopher shouted to him the night of the twentieth, "WHERE ARE YOU GOING? YOU CAN'T LEAVE NOW!" Micah turned and replied with a grin, "THEIR YOUR PEOPLE, NOT MINE. I AM ENGLISH REMEMBER, I AM HEADING NORTH TOWARDS JUANA, TO TALK TO THE PEOPLE THAT YOU HAVE LIED TO FOR THE PAST DECADE. LISTEN, IT WAS FUN, BUT

YOU HAVE NOT BEEN A GOOD MAN" Micah left and arrived at la Isabela on the last day of August. He built a raft and set sail toward Cuba. He changed his mind and sailed east first, arrived at Guadeloupe, and spoke to their people, giving them treasures stolen from Christopher's ship. He then sailed North West towards Haiti and fell asleep. A few days later, he awoke to find himself near land. Micah thought they were the Bahamas and turned west and soon landed on solid ground.

Micah stepped onto the rock to which he tied his raft and looked around. He took another step and went knee-deep into the swamp. He waded to solid ground, and after two hours of walking, he finally reached the solid ground only to find it still covered with water and trees. It was a swamp. Animals the likes of Mitchell had never seen swam and walked around the sandy ground he was standing on. Then he spotted long and narrow boats that floated along the rivers. A man and his lady turned and saw Micah and shouted in an unknown language. Micah waved, and they came closer. Micah saw when they were closer, they looked like the Arawak people but were taller slightly. They indicated to get in, and when he arrived at a village of people all dressed in the skin of what looked like a black cat. Micah ate with them since it was late and learnt their way. He pointed to a boat and asked if he could use one. They nodded, and that sunrise, he left the coast of what he thought was a swamp island and rowed east towards England. He continued to row, sometimes allowing the boat just to sail away. Micah thought of Christopher and how he would explain to the King about the little gold which was on the islands. He then fell asleep and dreamt of the people he met, and then the dream changed to a woman's voice saying, "Gelan, wake up, you are drowning."

Mitchell woke up underwater and swam up; he saw his boat upside down. He swam over and held on. He could not tell where he was and saw land ahead. He crashed a few hours later and found himself on Flores, a part of the Azores Archipelago. He woke up to see a group of girls and boys looking over him. He saw that his clothes were soaked and his pants were in tatters, but his legs showed no signs of a scratch. He asked the children for a boat, and they led him to their parents, and they gave him a boat. He asked for the day and was told it was October twentieth, and he realised he had spent almost a whole year on the sea. They watched him push off and sail towards the land of Spain. He passed Spain and used a pigeon (which was given to him by the islanders) and asked for his luggage in the Inn to be taken to Pisa. He arrived in the waters between Africa and France in

November. It wasn't until December thirty-first when he arrived in Pisa. He stepped into Port and spoke to a surprised Fisherman, "Excuse me can you tell me where Leonardo Da Vinci is?"

Farewell World, Welcome Rome

"Da Vinci, you say, and who are you to ask that?"

"My name is Michelangelo Greengrass, and I am told he has something to give me."

"He is on his way to Venice, going there because of the War."

"War?"

"A war between Louis the eighth of France and Ferdinand the second of Aragon."

"Right, I better be off then."

Michel left and headed towards Venice. He arrived in Mantua in February after shopping around for new clothes. He found him walking around, capturing the beauty. Michel called out, and Leonardo turned around and said, "And you are, my dear?"

"Michelangelo Greengrass, my father told me to come and collect items he made."

"And your father is?"

"Michael Green, my mother, fell pregnant the year fourteen sixty-nine, and I was born in January. My mother was young, and when I turned twenty, she died. I was living in Spain during the time when a pigeon told me to collect artwork; it was signed, Father."

"Luckily, they are with the rest of my belongings." Michel followed Leonardo to the house, and they arrived to see the table covered with drawings. Leonardo returned with the chess boards and pieces in a cloth bag and smiled. "These belonged to Michael."

"Chess, all he gave you were games of chess."

"Hand designed, and he gave me these as well." Leonardo pointed to the pictures; he drew from his past life.

"Can you teach me to paint?"

So, for a month, Michel was retaught how to paint and when they moved to Venice in March. While Leonardo was speaking to the Signoria about the Turkish incursion in Venice, Michel began a painting. During those months of painting, Michel learnt that Leonardo finished *Virgin of the Rocks, Lady with an Ermine, The Last Supper, La belle ferronnière*, Sala delle Asse, and Isabella Portrait *d'Este*. He was just finishing The Virgin and Child with St Anne and St John the Baptist. By the time they arrived in Florence. Michel continued with the faces of the four women, one with raven hair shoulder-length, eyes were green as fresh grass, he made them look aged to show being wise, the next was young with earth colour hair and eyes as amber as the fossil. Michel then painted another woman painted to be blind, and her dark hair was the same colour as the night sky. Michel's painting was nearly finished. As Michel painted the blue eyes of the sunshine blonde girl, Leonardo looked over his shoulder and asked, "Who are these women?"

"The women of my life are my mother, my first love, my first wife, and my guardian angel."

"Then I guess the name of this painting will be the four women of MG."

"Perfect."

Leonardo watched over Michel for four years, and then Michel left to explore Milan since the war was over.

It was June fifteen hundred four. When Michel passed Palazzo Della Signoria and saw the statue of David by Michelangelo, which stood seventeen feet high in the middle of the Palazzo Della Signoria. Michel walked out of the town and found a horse. He arrived in Milan and found the house, knowing that only sixteen years had passed so when he knocked, the door opened to a man with green eyes and brown hair smiled and said, "Sorry we are not interested in the war, I already lost my brother because of the war."

"I am not here for the war. My name is Michelangelo Greengrass; Michael was my father. I am wondering if I could speak to your Grandfather about something."

"He is a hundred and feeling ill. We fear he is going to die during this winter. So, if you wish to speak to him, sure, my father is out earning money. Since your dad found the letters, my dad was trying to crack the notebook's code, but so far, the words he has are strange."

Michel walked in to see a canvas of words, some complete, others weren't finished, and most started being written with encouragement. Michel walked in to see the once elderly man look ancient and pale.

"Son of Michael comes to see my final days." He mutters, voice hoarse with old age.

"I have come to either ease your mind or put wonderment into your mind before you die."

"What could you say that would do that?"

"I am Michael Green; I am also Magnus."

"If so, then promise me something. Promise me that you will look after our family and if the line of Julius dies, then you will live a happy life knowing that we are proud to have you as our original ancestor."

"Why aren't you in shock?"

"When I first saw you, I could tell that you were the same person, hair can change but not the eyes, you have passed down the green eyes from Julius down to my son, green eyes show that we are the same be proud of your family." The man breathed his last with a smile.

The young man walked in and said, "He was waiting for you, it seems; what did he say?"

"He told me to look after you without being rude. Which one are you?"

"Judas died when the soldiers attacked our city."

"Janus, I will watch over you." And when his father came home, Janus told his dad, and Michel lived under their roof for the next few months. Helping to decipher the code, it was spring when Michel turned to Janus and asked, "You with anyone?"

"Yes, but I am ashamed to go any further. She was my brother's fiancée."

"That's new," and suddenly the door opened and a young woman stepped through and said "Janus, I tried to visit, but your father said you are organising a funer…" she stopped and saw Michelangelo and asked, "Sorry, who are you?"

"Michel, I am a friend of the family."

"Nice to meet you. My name is Ruby."

"I will leave you to it," he whispered into Janus's ear, "If you love her, your brother will not mind." Michel left and rode the horse to the library. The next month was the funeral, and after that, Michel found out that Ruby had proposed to Janus, and he accepted. Michel was invited to the wedding.

The wedding was on February fourteenth, fifteen hundred five. Michel was sitting in the front row of the church. When Ruby walked to Janus, Michel had a flashback to his simple wedding to Paris and remembered how they lived happily. Michel snapped out of it when they took their vows, turned to the father, and whispered, "Listen, they make a lovely couple, and you will be fine."

The wedding was a success, and under orders, Michel stayed with the dad until the couple returned from Venice for their ten-week honeymoon. When they returned, Janus saw Michel and said, "Do you not have a home to return to?"

"I make my own home."

"You have no home, but what about your heir?"

"If I have an heir, it will be in the house of my love."

"Right!" Janus ran to his bedroom, and Ruby followed. Michel wrote a letter to Leonardo, and when it returned in March, Leonardo said, "I am in Florence. I am working on a portrait of Lisa del Giocondo, wife of Francesco del Giocondo. I am calling it Mona Lisa, and I haven't even began to capture her beauty. How is it going young Michelangelo, for the other Michelangelo has began working on the Pope's tomb, and another artist Raphael has began what he calls 'The *Ansidei Altarpiece*' and I suggest that if you can too visit him or at least one of your bloodlines for he is quite remarkable."

Michel wrote back, saying "I am with a friend at this present time. I will try to visit him. God be with you when you work on the Mona Lisa."

A month later, Ruby was smiling for she was with child, and the doctors were saying that Ruby was healthy. Michel drank with the father to the news and then spotted a word in the list of one hundred words, "I see the word 'letter' and the word 'Secundo' which is second in Latin."

"Secundo letter elute piano gamma", the father read out, mixing up the last of the letters and said, "Doesn't make sense!"

"Keep trying, but Secundo and letter keep them."

Michel then went over to Janus, who was looking worried, but he stopped and smiled when Michel walked in. "I am nervous; I am having a child with my brother's lover. I cannot continue like this."

"Stop this!" Michel raised his voice, and Janus stopped. "Remember your brother, name your first-born son Judas, and he will be happy, trust me, it is no point crying over the dead."

"Really?"

"Yes, now come on, let's play a game of chess; I will be black. Get out the present my father gave you."

Janus left and returned with the chessboard. With Ruby out with her parents, trying to get ready for the child, Janus was home without his wife. Janus opened the wooden box to reveal the Greek, and Roman gods, and out came a letter. It was in Judas's handwriting; Janus opened it up and cried, and he gave it to Michel to read. "Janus, if you are reading this, it means we haven't had a battle strategy in terms of chess. This means we have grown old, and we lost our childhood due to one thing, Ruby. We met her together one night, and she stole my heart as well as yours, but I think I did the wrong thing and removed her heart from her without her permission. I did wrong, I acted like you to attract her interest, and she was never into me, for she was into you. Ten years have passed, and she is wearing a ring that shows that she chose me over her heart. With this battle out there, I remembered chess and decided to leave you this last gift if I die, return Ruby's heart and make her happy."

Janus cried, and the father came in and saw the letter and spoke to Janus. "Guess Judas saw Ruby for who she was and gave her happiness."

In Judas's memory, Michel and Janus played chess, and the Romans beat the Greeks.

Christmas that year, Leonardo wrote a letter to Michel which read, "December fifteen hundred and five and what news I have I am nearly finished the portrait, I am still unhappy with the colour, that I will change. Raphael sent me sketches which I have attached, of his earliest paintings, some you might like; they are called 'The Mond Crucifixion', 'The Coronation of the Virgin', 'The Wedding of the Virgin' and 'Saint George and the Dragon' the last he did last year in Urbino. I will also be coming back to Milan in the next few months, so meet me at my old home…."

Michel replied, "I will travel to Florence next time you leave, for I will stay out of the house with the new baby."

After New Year and the moon was full in the sky, Ruby was nine months, and Janus was running around trying to help in any way possible. After two weeks, Ruby was in bed, and the men were outside while the midwives were helping with the delivery. Ruby was screaming, and minutes later, crying was heard. The door opened around sunset, and a girl was in Ruby's arms. Her eyes were bright blue, and Micah remembered the words of the dying man "You have passed down the green eyes from Julius down to my son; green eyes show that we are the same. Be proud of your family." And realised that the girl was from Ruby's family too and her eyes could be different colours. Ruby smiled and said, "Welcome to your family Prima Scarlet Tempus-Glorius named for being the first to join the Gloriuses and the Tempuses together."

She looked up and said, "Michel will you be the Godfather, I know it is a big ask, but I know you will do well."

Michel was shocked. His face faded, and the energy died when it dawned on him, "I can't; I might never be there when she wants me!"

Ruby smiled and laughed. "Someone will watch over her, it might not be Michelangelo, but it will be someone" she then beckoned Michel over and whispered, "I can see it in your eyes. You will be around to watch over, you have Janus's eyes, older, wiser and deeper as in you bear a great burden, but you will guide Janus and my daughter's family with your presence" she then spoke to the rest of the family "Greengrass will be Godfather" she winked. Michel realised she joined the dots and, like the Grandfather, found the truth.

On their anniversary, Michel left to meet Leonardo. Leonardo brought the Mona Lisa and Michel's painting and said, "Shall I keep this?"

"Better you have it than me. Someday, someone will collect it."

"Sure, I have something for you to keep; I made it based on my sketches of inventions." Leonardo pulled out an arm-length rod of metal. "It cannot corrode," Leonardo said, "I saw a few of your sketches and created a rod passed on what I saw; take it, it expands."

"How?"

"With a lever and spring system, just flick that switch, and it comes body length."

Michel flicked the switch, and sure enough, the rod tripled in size. "How do you shrink it?"

"Push it hard; it will shrink back. The grip is a cowskin and tree sap combination to protect yours from heat.

"Thank you," Michel gestured and spotted an engraving on the metal on either side of the grip and switch. "What does this say…" he stopped and used the sunlight to read the words "Mente ergo potentior est gladius," Michel stopped and translated ", The Mind is mightier than the sword."

"Correct, brainpower wins any battle."

Michel stayed with Leonardo for a year while working on 'The Virgin and Child with St Anne and St John the Baptist'. When Leonardo left for Florence, he was almost finished the 'The Madonna of the Yarnwinder', and with that, Micah returned to the nearly one-year-old Prima with his staff of metal.

Michel sent letters to Leonardo that year and continued to live with the Tempus family. When the baby was two, Leonardo returned to show Michel the pleased result of the Mona Lisa and news of Michelangelo, his namesake. Michel left the Tempus to visit Leonardo at Porta Orientale in the parish of Santa Babila. Leonardo brought news of Michelangelo and was given the honour of painting the ceiling of the Sistine Chapel. Michel decided to wait until Prima was older before heading back to Rome; there, we would also visit Raphael. Leonardo was surprised but shrugged this off when Michel spoke about the Tempuses. Leonardo enjoyed playing chess against Michel and asked if it was in the blood of the Greens to know chess. Michel just smiled and said, "guess so".

With the next few years passing and Prima learning to walk and talk, soon she was five, and Janus was thinking of trying to have a boy. Michel worked on the farms and used dirt and dust to hide that he still looked thirty-five. Ruby continued to smile as he walked in covered with dust, said, "Same old Michel", and laughed as if she knew his secret.

One night he asked her, "What do you know of me?"

"I know you pretend to be someone you are not. You lie and cover the truth with dirt. I may be getting older, I am thirty-seven, and you, Michel, haven't grown an inch since I first saw you."

"Stopped growing," Michel told the truth, but he meant it differently

"I think so; you are a mystery. Maybe that's why you can help with the book Janus will get in eleven years."

Soon it was Christmas Eve, and Michel was outside the house and could hear Janus and Ruby trying to have a son. It wasn't until New Year when they found out they were successful, and by then, Prima was nearly six. When Michel was told by Leonardo that Michel had nearly finished the ceiling. Raphael has completed a number of portraits such as Saint Catherine of Alexandria, Deposition of Christ, Portrait of Elisabetta Gonzaga, and Portrait of Pope Julius II. Michel replied, "I will try to get there, hopefully."

It was soon Prima's sixth birthday, and it was confirmed that Ruby was pregnant when she was sick. Michel gave her a wooden doll, and they went back to helping the father with the notebook since he was out learning archery under the orders of the King. Months passed, and soon Ruby was in labour on the morning of the twenty-ninth of September. Judas Midas Tempus-Glorius was born, and Michel went over to Ruby and said, "I am not going to be able to be Godfather for both, you know why. I will try to watch over her family with mine, but there is no promise I can do both."

"I know. That's why I got you only to look after my daughter's side. Promise me you will try."

"I will try."

For the next year, Michel left for the Vatican and arrived a week later in October. He first made sure he looked old and arrived at the Sistine Chapel. The sight of the artwork took Michel's breath away, and walking around the building was like looking into a canvas of living colour. Michel prayed to the Lord for such gifts, and then a young voice spoke, "Not bad for a thirty-eight-year-old, but that was a year ago now, all dry."

"Who might you be to critic such beauty," Michel said, turning around

"Raphael, eight years younger but still famous, and who are you, old-timer? Your hairs are as white as ash?"

"Michelangelo Greengrass."

"The apprentice of Leonardo, the painter of the four women of MG, well nice to make your acquaintance, shame you arrived this late; you are getting older by the day."

"Why the other Michelangelo is still working on the coffin for the Pope."

"True, and I just finished the Galatea last year."

After that, Raphael took Michel to an inn, and they had a meal and talked, "Where is Leonardo can I visit?"

"He is working for the Pope, unable to be disturbed at his old age. Shame you are younger than him. He met your father when they were around the same age, both brilliant."

For the next few years, under the rule of King Henry the eighth and Pope Leo the tenth, Raphael and Michel talked, and Michel watched as Raphael finished a few other arts. Easter was drawing near. Raphael commented, "I was born on Friday the twenty-eighth of March, which happened to be Good Friday."

They got word from Leonardo that he would be leaving for France soon, and he sent God's love to them. For the next three years, Michel continued to age but began to put on a show. He used the staff Leonardo gave him as a walking stick to pretend he was getting old, and when it was May, a letter came from France saying that Leonardo had passed away. Michel cried for a week and continued to help Raphael in any way. He travelled wherever Raphael went. They spoke about Leonardo and how he was a genius and how the Mona Lisa will be well known. They parted ways around January fifteen-twenty, and a few months later, a young lady arrived at the inn where Michel was staying. He was getting ready to move to France when the woman stood at his door and said, "Raphael is dead. He gave me this to give to you, he passed away on Good Friday and had enough time to write his will, but he also wrote this."

"Michelangelo Greengrass: I Raphael give you this sketch in which I made of what I call the five artists of the Renaissance. I wish you to find Michelangelo your namesake and tell him to make us artists proud. Your friend R."

Michel went to the funeral and watched the artwork be given to their new owners and, after a while, left to find Michelangelo. Using the staff as a walking stick, Michelangelo pretended to be twenty years older and arrived in Florence to see Michelangelo aged and annoyed at his new orders for the tomb, which he spent twelve years on. Michel decided to not interrupt and left for Milan, he arrived there to find the place changed, but once he found the home of the Tempuses, he knocked to find Janus's father, old and tired.

"Michel, they moved out, they live somewhere around here, just ask around they left when Judas was three. Michel finally found the home and saw the teenage Prima dancing with her younger brother. Ruby spotted him and said, "Still acting. When will you give up and show who you are?"

"I can't if I do, it will be the end of me. I have to hide my true colours. Listen, I am leaving for France soon. I will change, but I promise to keep an eye on your daughter in the future."

"You better!" She led him indoors. To Michel's surprise, Janus was happy to see him. The bow and arrow showed that he followed his father with the archery, and they had dinner.

Michel stayed for the next two years to be there when Janus received the notebook and the list of words Michel and the father put together. He smiled and said, "this code has taken a while, but with your help, Michel, it will be cracked."

Michel then decided to stay until Judas's thirteenth birthday or just after, so when Judas turned thirteen in the year fifteen twenty-five, Prima was three quarters of a year before her twentieth, and Michel decided to see his Goddaughter turn twenty. After Christmas that year, Michel went over to Prima and spoke to her, "Listen, I am your Godfather. I give you this ring, it belonged to my….call her my love, take this ring. I already asked your mother, and she said yes, this ring after being blessed by her, will be a sign of my love, wherever I am, but here's the thing, your mother already guessed it. You must only tell your children they cannot pass it on to anyone but theirs. You must tell them that they have one Godfather whose love will endure forever."

Prima looked up and said, "Godfather, are you saying you will watch over in spirit or flesh and blood?"

"That is the scary part. I will be doing both. Promise you won't tell your brother, he is already named after a dead uncle, and I promised your mother I would look after your family."

"I promise," she said.

Michel prepared for his journey to France. After her birthday, Michel left on the first of February and started walking toward the French border. It was the year twenty-six, and Michel found a new name for himself. Merlin Grace would be his new identity once he crossed the border; he headed towards Lyon. Once Merlin was out of Milan and in the town of Vercelli, he washed the ash out of his hair and turned back to his young self. He changed clothes and placed the staff in the backpack. He was young again and left. He then arrived in Turin four days later and was spotted and claimed to be a criminal. Merlin then was then taken to Germany for his alias Merlin Grace was similar to a crook named Medwin Graze, a serial killer during that time. Merlin (Mitchell) was taken to Germany from there for execution. After a month of walking, stopping only for a day at Berne and Zurich, Mitchell arrived in Munich, where he was sentenced to death by archery. After a year in prison, Mitchell was tied and stood back to the archers and was asked for any last requests, and Mitchell replied: "That my belongings and I be placed in a box in a river Oder."

"Very well, Fire!"

The arrows went straight through Mitchell's body, and they claimed him dead, but on his travels to Berlin to be dropped in the river, his body had no injuries when they were halfway there and being tied to the horse made Mitchell groan. They rushed to Berlin to claim him of witchcraft, and they decided to burn him at the stake. After arriving there in June fifteen, twenty-eight was asked for his last request, and the same was what he said "Place me in the river Oder" his belongings and shirt were tossed into the box, and once they burned Mitchell, his blackened body was sealed in, Mitchell waited for him to hear the splash and he held his breath. After a while, his body healed, and he heard the sound of open water. He broke the box with the staff and saw him in the middle of the Baltic Sea. He saw Szczecin in the distance and realised he had arrived on the wrong side of Denmark. He began to row towards Denmark. For forty days, Mitchell was in the sea eating raw fish and drinking saltwater. He finally arrived on the shores of Aberdeen.

Merlin spent years living in a cave with flamed fish and salted water to eat and drink. His beard grew, and so did his hair. During the next nineteen years, while King Henry married his first wife and Mary was born, Merlin saw the comet and lived in the cave from the time of Henry's other wives, the births of Elizabeth, Henry and Edward. Merlin's hair was covered with sand and ash, turned light with sunlight, and became white. Merlin lived to pass the march of Pizarro from Panama to Peru. After nineteen years, Merlin counted the years off with each passing fireworks in the sky. Merlin decided to sleep for a while to allow his body to process the raw fish and saltwater, for his body was strong, but his system was weak.

Feeling the Love, Drama and Pain

Merlin woke up and walked towards town. His sun-bleached hair, turned white, was down to his chest and back, reflecting the light to give him a holy glow. He walked up with his staff to help get a grip when he reached the top of the cliff to see a bunch of people staring at him. He had a suitcase in one hand and a staff in the other. His clothes were wet and ragged, and his green eyes were glowing with energy. The boy asked him, "Who are you traveller that comes after the death of our beloved King Henry and the reign of his son Edward?"

"My name is Merlin…."

"Merlin, the great wizard?"

"No, I am Merlin Grace, I would like to find an inn to wash and eat, and I have been camping for a while and need a comfy bed."

A man spoke from behind the boy, "I will show you the way; you arrive in a time of great mourning and a great victory, for he was cruel."

When Merlin arrived at the inn, he requested for two pigeons to arrive, so he could send letters. He wrote a letter saying that I am Michel Greengrass. I am dying, but I wish to hear from the family of Tempus living in Italy. He then sent another letter to Michelangelo with the sketch he was given by Raphael. After a few days of living in the inn, a pigeon returned it was from Judas it said "Been twenty-one years since we have heard from you, my father who is in his seventies thought you have died, but my sister said you will write, we are both married, and my sister has a daughter named Scarlet, and we have a son named Leo. Prima is expecting twins, and we are thinking of having another in a few years. In sixteen years, the notebook will be given to me or when my father dies. He wishes you had spoken to us sooner, but my mother Ruby is glad you are out there in the world." Merlin cried and replied, "Thank you, I had a son after I left. His children might visit yours depending on how we go. If not, his descendent will try to visit yours, Michelangelo Greengrass."

That was the end of Michel Greengrass, and Merlin walked out of the inn three years later to find the rule under King Edward still bloody.

When Merlin left for the city of Dundee to find a job, the rumours were that the Act of Uniformity had removed the icons and statues of the saints and whitewashed over wall paintings, as well as the fact that the Duke of Somerset was deposed as Protector of England, and is replaced by John Dudley, Earl of Warwick who creates himself Duke of

Northumberland. He arrives in Dundee and gets a job as a carpenter, where he helps build chairs for the United Kingdom houses. After a few years of working there, Merlin hears word that the Duke of Northumberland is trying to persuade Edward to nominate his daughter-in-law Lady Jane Grey as his heir. Still, Edward died before he could decide, leaving the throne to what seemed to be Lady Jane Grey as Queen, but Merlin found out on the first of October that his half-sister Mary arrived in London and arrested Lady Jane Grey and was crowned Queen. Merlin continued to work, and the word was out that Queen Mary intended to marry Philip of Spain. Merlin leaves for Glasgow to deliver some furniture and arrives at Glasgow to hear that Sir Thomas Wyatt, Lady Jane Grey, and her husband are executed. Mary sent Princess Elizabeth to the Tower of London on suspicion of involvement in Wyatt's rebellion. Merlin lives in Glasgow for a year and, on his return to Dundee, heard rumours and stories of Elizabeth's release and the Protestant bishops being burned at the stake. Merlin arrives back in Dundee and is paid well. He returns to Aberdeen; there, he goes into hiding by leaving for the cave. For the next few years, he lies low, and in the year fifteen hundred and fifty-eight, when Queen Bloody Mary is dead after being persuaded to declare war against France was when Marvin Grace comes out from the caves with hair longer and fresh clothes. He headed straight for Glasgow to catch a carriage to London and find a job or work around England. During the travel, Marvin heard that Queen Elizabeth would be crowned in January, a month away. Marvin arrived in London and was there for the coronations. He worked as a painter for the Queen, for his talents were spotted when he painted the scene of her coronation. He was inside the castle and was paid very little for his art. After a few years, when Mary Queen of Scot declared herself Queen of France, Scotland and England and Elizabeth was named Head of Church of England, Queen Elizabeth founded Westminster School, and Marvin was transferred there as a teacher of the arts.

Marvin works as a teacher of arts for the next two decades from fifteen sixty to fifteen eighty at the school, while England around him changes. People died from the Plague after troops occupied Dieppe and Le Havre to aid in the French Wars of Religion. The count reached seventeen thousand. After that, peace was made between England and France at Troyes and potatoes and tobacco were brought from the New World, which Marvin promised not to touch the tobacco. Mary Queen of Scots flees to England from Scotland and is imprisoned by Elizabeth. It was the year fifteen seventy-four when Marvin was given a new student, one from Stratford, Marvin saw the talent he had, and when he returned three years later, Marvin caught his name Shakespeare, Son of High Bailiff John Shakespeare and then Marvin received a letter to paint on the voyage of the globe. Still, he declined to join Francis Drake on his trip to navigate the globe, and Marvin found out Drake was knighted a year later when he returned.

It was the year fifteen eighty-five when Marvin was no longer a teacher and pretended to be older than he was. Marvin was walking around London to see a young man around writing on parchment, muttering inaudible words. Marvin went over and said, "Well, haven't I seen you before." The man looked up and said, "Possibly, I've only been here once before. My name is William."

"Shakespeare, you were one of my students."

"You are the art teacher. I can see it in your face. I don't forget a face."

"Likewise, so William, what brings you here?"

"I am looking for inspiration to write plays."

"Plays, well then I have a place for you if you like; I know a house out of town full of inspiration. Belonged to the famous Gelan."

"To be honest, I never heard of him."

"Then maybe the house will ring some bells."

Marvin led William to the house in Hastings after a week's journey by horse, stopping for the nights they arrived, and when William stepped in, he said, "What the dickens!" and then wrote that down, saying, "I might use that!"
Marvin hadn't stepped inside the house for a few centuries, and the wall was covered with dust, but his old home's vibe was still here.

"Looks like it has been deserted, but that would have been ages ago. This place holds many stories. I can just sense all this energy, mind, if I stay here for a while."

"Sure, I will go to town and buy some food; I will send a letter to my son so he can mind the house."

For the next four and a half years, William Shakespeare wrote letters to his wife and kids, and as he did this wrote ideas after ideas and tossed them in the fire. It wasn't until Marvin arrived one morning and said, "Stop wasting the paper. Listen, have I told you about Milan and the people I know from there? Trust me, some are lovebirds just asking women out."

William Shakespeare looked up and said, "Thank you, I have got it." He left for London after a stop at the library in Hastings. He looked around and saw a few interesting things and then took the carriage to London. Marvin shouted after him, "My son will see you around." Mitchell began to walk to

London, following a hidden route. He arrived a week after William and got word that William was writing a play about King Henry. When Marvin as Marvelo arrived to see him, William looked at Marvin's art and said, "The object of art is to give life a shape, and I think you have just shown us that life is messy and complicated." William turned and said, "You look like your father; something about him is in you. I just can't put my finger on it."

Marvelo helped William with his plays for the next few years and helped him get his history right for his plays Henry the sixth, one, two and three. One morning in the year ninety-two, while William was writing Richard the third, Marvelo walked in and said, "You got the name wrong it is Anne, not Anna", and she died by a poison drink, not food."

"You know this how?"

"I live for the past and present."

"I can see that. Your eyes tell the story as if you were there to see it or believe it with your own eyes."

After that, Marvelo left Shakespeare and returned to Dundee for a few years. While this was happening, William performed his plays on stage.

It was the morning of fifteen ninety-six around August when a letter from Shakespeare saying that his only son passed away because of the plague, and the funeral was on the eleventh. Marvelo arrived in London to see the whole town buzzing about his plays The Comedy of Errors, Love's Labour's Lost, Richard the second, Romeo and Juliet and A Midsummer Night's Dream, word of others included Titus Andronicus, Richard the third, Edward the third, some of which Marvelo helped him in. He arrived at an inn and found William depressed and in a writing frantic. He saw Marvelo and said, "We know what we are, but not what we may be, for you look like your father with your hair long, and you look like him in every way. I will work out this mystery as for me to weep is to make less the depth of grief."

"Hope you are writing these down," Marvelo joked and then saw how he was and tried to help. We saw the pages of a half-written script of Love's Labour's Won. William pushed it aside and said, "Have you lost anyone like I have? Have you lost a loved one?"

"Yes, I did, years ago, I lost my mother, my love, even my family, but as you know, I am different. I am fighting a curse."

"Curse, you fight a curse, while I fight a broken heart." The papers went flying as William went mad. He turned the inn upside down and soon, he was taken to Bethlem. Marvelo picked up the papers and saw the script for a play called "The man that walked the earth", and it was about a man that walked the earth, it was about Mitchell, he saw that it was rewritten over and over again and the papers were a mess. Marvelo grabbed them and placed them in his pocket. After a while, as William was writing plays in hospital, Marvelo was asked to help decorate the new theatre. It wasn't until fifteen ninety-nine that William asked Marvelo to help perform his plays on the big stage, saying, "The world's a stage and all the men and women merely players; they have their exits and their entrances; one man in his time plays many parts, so I suggest you live a little and act for you don't know this could be the first time for something."

For the next few years, Marvelo acted in the plays from the first plays he wrote; playing lead roles, Marvelo learnt all ways of acting and drama. First, Marvelo was Nicholas in Taming of the Shrew, Margaret in King Henry all three and that made the audience laugh, especially when Marvelo was crowned Queen Margaret. When Marvelo played Queen Margaret as a widow in the King Richard play, everyone was shocked to see a familiar face for the same role but cried at his lines. His role in Richard II was minor, and his role as King Philip's son was a really hard part, considering Marvelo had to remember what he learnt about Louis the Dauphin. It was three years since the Globe had been built when Marvelo spoke to William, saying, "I am going home, my son is nearly thirty, and I am in my fifties. I better see him before he finds the love of his life."

William turned and spoke, "Men at some time are masters of their fates. The fault, dear Marvelo, is not in our stars, but in ourselves, that we are underlings."

"That's from Caesar. You are taking words from your own play to me. Come on, can't you think of something new?"

"All's well if all ends well, and that reminds me, I now know why you look like your father. If you cut your hair, you will be exactly like him. You are either a clone or the same person with long hair."

"A line from your own play 'So wise and so young, you say, do never live long?' but in my guess 'So old and so wise', remember the curse I spoke of, well you saw it too, I am as you said so in Merchant of Venice "If you prick us, do we not bleed? If you tickle us, do we not laugh? If you poison us, do we not die? And if you wrong us, shall we not revenge? Well, if you prick me, I do not bleed. If you poison me, I do not die. I will live on as long as my body is given oxygen and sunlight."

"Can it not be reversed?"

"What's done cannot be undone! Take that you might use it someday."

"Seriously, you are being honest, for you know; Honesty is the best policy."

"If I was being dishonest, would this be a trick of the eye."
Marvelo stabbed himself with a knife in the arm and pulled it
out to reveal the blood on the blade, but that was all. The
wound was open and healing slowly but quicker than a
normal person. "Promise me, you will not tell a soul. I will
return in three years or around that as my son, with shorter
hair and different clothes. You must act like you never have
seen me, and you just met for the first time."

"This above all: to thine own self be true, and I promise I
would not tell as soul, for I Listen to many and speak to a few
when it comes to something of the unusual."

Marvelo left, and William edited his Hamlet play by adding a
line, "There are more things in heaven and earth, Horatio,
than are dreamt of in your philosophy." And then smiled and
said, "there is more to than meets the eye when it comes to
people."

Around sixteen hundred and four, Marvelo returned
as a new person, with his old stuff inside the bag and the
staff as an heirloom. He arrived at the Globe as Mervyn Grace
and asked to speak to the author after watching the play
Hamlet been played on stage. William came and said, "You
must be the son of Marvelo. Come on in. I need to talk about
your father."

Inside, William turned and said, "What is it, kind sir?"

"What does that line mean? "There are more things in heaven and earth, Horatio, than are dreamt of in your philosophy?"

"You will see, for you are one of them, and everyone will believe it is just another clever line of mine."

Mervyn stayed in a room opposite Shakespeare's inn in the town of Southwark. Shakespeare continued to write as his daughters grew up. Some years Mervyn would organise a party just to celebrate their birthdays. It was 1607, and it was the beginning of June when word came from his oldest daughter Susanna saying she was engaged. They took a carriage together to Holy Trinity Church. They arrived just in time, a day before the wedding. William turned towards Mervyn in the carriage and said, "Don't get any ideas about falling for my girls. They can take care of themselves; just because you look thirty doesn't mean you can...."

"I am older than you think, and trust me, after my first love died, I will not marry again."

"Thank the Lord for that," William said as they arrived. They took their seats and watched as Susanna married John Hall, a thirty-two-year-old physician. Shakespeare's wife was there, Anne Hathaway and his daughter Judith, aged twenty-two. After the reception, Shakespeare was told that Susanna was expecting a baby. During the next few months, Shakespeare wrote a play called "All's Well That Ends Well", and Mervyn stayed in Stratford-upon-Avon for the same period. It was soon Judith's twenty-third birthday. Susanna was really chubby and nearly thirty-eight weeks. Mervyn had permission to dance with the birthday girl and his eldest daughter. After the party, Mervyn headed off to an inn, and three weeks later, around the twenty-first, William was looking into the eyes of his grandchild. Elizabeth Hall cried in the arms of her grandfather and mother. Mervyn whispered into the ears of Shakespeare, "see you back in London," and he left.

Back in London, King James got word that the men who arrived in America somehow managed to lose over fifty-one of the settlers who lived a year in Jamestown, which was found by the Virginia company. Shakespeare returned and began working on his new plays. He was happier than he was when Hamnet died, and Mervyn was glad that the marriage and the birth of Elizabeth inspired William to write more. That only lasted four years. He picked up a partner, and Mervyn was just the historian. After Elizabeth's fourth birthday, Mervyn's services were required to check the realism of the play Henry the eighth, or 'All is True'. But that was the last play he wrote, he finished 'The Two Noble Kinsmen' before he finished Henry the Eighth, and once it was done, he moved back towards Stratford-upon-Avon so he could be close to his family. Another few years had passed and the year was sixteen fifteen and nearly New Year's Eve when Mervyn received a letter inviting him to the New Year celebration at Stratford-upon-Avon. Mervyn left and arrived that night for the fireworks show.

The next few months, Mervyn was treated as a guest, and when Judith, aged thirty-one, got married to a twenty-seven-year-old Thomas Quiney, a vintner of Stratford. Mervyn watched Shakespeare and noticed that he wasn't looking depressed. After finding out that the wedding was not legit, Mervyn left for the home of Shakespeare to find him already told and was editing the will after Thomas confessed to sleeping with another woman during their engagement, and she died during labour. Mervyn sat while Shakespeare changed the will and then looked up and said, "You already got something. You do not need it written down. You have a play of mine, lost all those years ago during my madness. Keep it and look after my children." Shakespeare passed away the following month, and Mervyn was in the background during the funeral. He went over to the site and read the words on the tomb "Good friend, for Jesus' sake forbear, to dig the dust enclosed here. Blessed be the man that spares these stones, and cursed be he that moves my bones." Mervyn then lived in that town and kept his promise to watch over his family. He watched as Judith gave birth to a boy and was named Shakespeare. He watched as Susanna and John lived with Elizabeth, now eight. Mervyn was called over to the house of Judith when Shakespeare was ill and asked if he could take him to the hospital because she was not feeling up to going. Thomas looked over her, and Mervyn left. He saw the dying eyes of the boy and then remembered the underwater caves in Aberdeen and the frozen walls and wondered. He took Shakespeare to the Hospital and found out that he was minutes away from death. He returned home saying he was dead after giving him a solution of a liquid made from the digitalis leaf, and Judith cried. However, after the burial, Mervyn returned and took the boy to the caves of Aberdeen during the night he travelled, and he arrived and gave the boy a kiss and whispered, "You will be cured. You aren't dead yet." The baby's eyes opened and then closed as he fell asleep the solution he gave the boy wore off. Mervyn buried him in the icy walls and said, "I will return when the time is safe. I will block the cave and make sure you will not be disturbed. I promised to keep your family safe which I will do."

Mervyn used the rocks to block the cave entrance and wrote on a rock saying, "Here lies Merlin, the old, step inside and be cursed."

Mervyn watched the birth of the next two boys of Judith and was at Anne's funeral and watched as her daughters wept over the grave. Judith was now thirty-eight, and the boys were toddlers. Susanna was around forty, and her daughter Elizabeth was fifteen. Elizabeth spotted a man that looked like Mervyn but decided it was his son. As the years passed, Mervyn was there at the funeral of Judith's sons, aged nineteen and twenty-one, Elizabeth was there for her mother, and after placing roses, she looked around and spotted Mervyn and walked over after everyone left and asked: "Are you the son of my grandfather's friend, Mervyn?"

"I am M" Mitchell froze, he was meant to be hiding, yet Elizabeth spotted him twice, and he didn't look seventy.

"Malin and yes I am his son." Mitchell lied and watched as Elizabeth processed it.

"Came here to pay your respects, are you?" Elizabeth said, stepping closer, her brown hair floating in the breeze, and her breath was warm on his skin.

"Yes", Malin stuttered, taking a step back, but Elizabeth stepped forward and whispered, "Why are you sweating?"

"Because you are awfully close to a single man, yet you wear a ring, my lady."

"I was young then and was foolish, the marriage has lasted thirteen years, but he was royal, can't I just for once have someone my own age."

"Sorry, my Lady, but my father promised that our family can't get involved with yours."

"But your father isn't here, and neither is Shakespeare."

"I am terribly sorry," Malin mumbled and ran away towards the houses. He turned to see Elizabeth watch him for a minute and then walk away.

Malin went to his room and began to cry and then saw the play in his suitcase and began to read the lines that Shakespeare wrote about a man who walked the earth. Grabbing paper and a quill, Malin began to write. He wrote about his childhood, he wrote about the Roman fights, he wrote about his trip to England and the fights, and he wrote about the trip with Columbus. Malin wrote six hundred pages, some in Latin, some in Italian and the rest in English. He bound the book and then found a wooden box and stuffed everything, the play, the book, the clothes, the musty pages of the play Labour's Love Won, and he even placed the few trophies of the past century, including the chess boards and pieces, leaving only his staff, the undershirt, the necklace and that was it. He went to town and bought new clothes before going back to his room, sealing the box with rope, and writing a note saying "Past life of MG." The year was sixteen forty-seven, and Malin left for Hastings. He arrived in Hastings around May twentieth, and he went to his house, dug up the floor and dug a hole in the hill. He buried the box and then burned the house after making sure all items of worth were in the hole too. The house ashes covered the newly filled hole, and when he walked away, the house turned to dust and ash.

Malin arrived in Stratford around April tenth to find his hotel door ajar. He opened to see a lovely lady sitting on his bed, looking at the staff and trying to figure out the writing and design. The lady dropped the staff when Malin stood in the doorway and turned and said, "Sorry, I was told this was your room. I only have been here for nearly a week." "Elizabeth Nash, what are you doing in my room?" "Waiting for you, I would like to know about my grandfather; I was young when he died, after all." Malin told her what he knew, pretending it was passed down from his father and grandfather. Elizabeth came closer and held his hand when he told about changing the will just for you and then stopped when she was nearly sitting on his lap.

"Elizabeth, I told you once, I cannot do this. You are married, and my family swore an oath."

"I am a widow. My husband died last week and left me his meadows. I am alone and miserable, for I fell for an older man."

Malin hugged her and said, "There is someone out there for everyone." He helped her out of the room and watched as she left in tears. Malin's heart ached with the memories of his first love and the life he brought living with the curse.

Months passed, and Malin was invited to Elizabeth's wedding, for she decided to marry again. This time to a younger man called John Barnard, and a month later, he was invited to the funeral of Susanna, and he wrote on her tombstone a message fit for a playwright's daughter "Here lyeth the body of Susanna, wife of John Hall, gent., the daughter of William Shakespeare, gent. She deceased on the 11th day of July, Anno 1649, aged 66. Witty above her sex, but that's not all, Wise to Salvation was good Mistress Hall, Something of Shakespeare was in that, but this. Wholly of him with whom she's now in blisse.

Then, passenger, hast nere a tear. To weep with her that wept with all

That wept, yet set herself to chere. Them up with comforts cordiall?

Her love shall live, her mercy spread. When thou hast nere a tear to shed."

Malin then stayed in his inn since Elizabeth moved to New Place after inheriting the house of Shakespeare. Malin hid from Elizabeth's sight at the funeral of Judith after another thirteen years had passed. She had outlived her own children by twenty-three years. Malin lived on even up to the death of Elizabeth in the year sixteen seventy. Malin then changed again and headed for Hastings before living for another thirty years. He caught a boat to the mainland and headed towards a city he knew from childhood, and from stories of the war, he headed towards France.

Many jobs for the Baroque

Malin arrived in the town of Brest as Matthieu Gaston and walked to an inn. He spent all his money getting on the boat and was totally broke. He went to bed that night, thinking of what he could possibly do. That night he dreamt of a girl with sunshine blonde hair she was around his age and was standing in a library, she spoke in a low voice, he walked over and heard her say "This can't be real, can a man really walk around Europe."

Matthieu woke up and realised it was a memory. He was about to change clothes when he realised that he had nothing but the necklace and staff and decided to find a job. First, Matthieu walked down the busy streets of Brest after borrowing some clothes and saw a stall needing a paint job. And Matthieu walked over and asked politely in French, "Excusez-moi, voulez-vous que je repeindre votre stand?" The owner smiled and said "Oui, s'il vous plaît." Mattheiu found some paints and got to work. He asked the owner, "Couleurs?"

"Rose Red, jaune soleil." The owner replied

Matthieu got out the two colours and began to paint, it was early in the morning, and people gathered around to see the work after a few hours. Soon the stall looked like roses in the sunshine, and the owner was pleased. Suddenly Matthieu heard a dozen voices shout out, "Moi la prochaine, pas moi, peindre ma maison, mon toit." (Me next, no me, paint my house, my roof)

Matthieu was busy for the next year, painting houses, stalls and even portraits; after a year of painting, a man in a uniform appeared and shouted in French, "Tous les hommes âgés de 30 à 40 doivent s'inscrire pour défendre notre pays."

When May arrived, Matthieu was given the uniform and told to travel to Spain to help protect the country from the Allies. Matthieu obeyed and travelled and joined the others a fortnight later. Arriving on the coast of Spain in a town called Barcelona in the area of Catalonia. The Allies arrived from the north and from their boats. Others rode horseback with swords and shields. With the sound of the horn and the orders from the leader, Matthieu charged. He packed his staff just in case but held the sword he was given as he galloped towards his own kin. Matthieu didn't know if any of his family was fighting, and as he saw the first soldier drop to the ground dead, Matthieu threw the sword away and jumped on the horse and pulled out the staff. Matthieu stood up and shouted in Latin, "Domine, remitte mihi, Walter consanguineos doleo." which meant O Lord, forgive me, Walter's relatives, I am sorry. Since Matthieu was on the horse, he stood higher than the others and with one flick of the switch, he extended the staff and started to disarm the Allies and shouted in English, "Fall back, I cannot stop what the French and Spanish do."

A British soldier spoke as his sword flew out of his hand.

"Why would you care about us? You are French?"

"My parents are French, but I was raised in England," Matthieu told the soldier the truth to some extent. But the soldier shrugged and charged onwards, picking up his sword and screaming as the opposition killed him. Matthieu continued to warn the Allies as he disarmed them using Leonardo's staff, and as they foolishly ignored him, Matthieu remembered the words of the staff "The mind is mightier than the sword."

The number of casualties was upsetting, and after a year in battle, with weekends to rest and heal (Matthieu was unscathed even with his foolish stunt), the total of soldiers still fighting reached for France was two hundred fifty-five thousand with eighteen thousand Spanish against a total of two hundred thirty-two thousand with forty thousand being from the Kingdom of England. With the death of William, the King of England, Queen Anne was still declaring war and Eugene of Savoy had left for Italy, giving Matthieu no choice but to follow.

Matthieu arrived in Italy to find that Duc de Villeroi had been captured. Matthieu rushed to the house of the Tempus to find it empty and dusty. He looked inside and noticed that no one lived here for at least fifty years and realised that with Prima and Judas both married with kids when he wrote they both would not have been living in the same house, he didn't ask in the letter for they must have been scattered. Praying they were safe and well, he went into battle and warned the Roman Empire and the French that they would all be in his wrath if one more body dropped dead. They laughed and charged onwards. Matthieu disarmed many English and Dutch soldiers, but all were foolish to take his words as the fight continued. Matthieu returned to France, bringing back injured soldiers.

After two years of fighting against his own kin, Matthieu got orders from the French to go to the Low Country to capture the Duke of Marlborough. The march took over one hundred and fifty hours, and by the time they arrived, the Dutch and English were moving away from the Netherlands and towards Germany. With orders, the army charged after them and, after three days of a chase, arrived in Germany, where they battled for a month until the Dutch fled with their men. They charged after them, with the dead being left behind, Matthieu charged ahead and was a target for many arrows, but they were not alive to know what kept him riding. After days of charging, they arrived back in the South of Germany, where the men of Eugene waiting. The combined armies of what was left of Germany began a battle. Mathieu disarmed and knocked out the men on the thirteenth of August, but the Allies were winning, for they had the Austrians now with them with more guns than them. They still ended up defeating twenty thousand due to drowning, death by bullet or sword, and many with serious injuries. They had captured over fourteen thousand. Matthieu counted the dead on the other side and saw less than a fifth of ours were dead and over seven thousand were, retreating, injured.

With the loss of the Bavarians, the next year was a complete stalemate, with attempts to intrude being turned empty-handed. The next year, Matthieu went through, and after seeing blonde angel three times, once in Blenheim and twice again in Ramillies and Turin, Matthieu reflected on how the stalemate ended with Marlborough driving out the French from most of the Spanish Netherlands, decisively defeating troops under Villeroi in the Battle of Ramillies during May and then following up with the conquest of Antwerp and Dunkirk. Prince Eugene also succeeded in September, following the departure of Vendôme, to shore up the shattered army in the Netherlands. He and the Duke of Savoy inflicted a heavy loss on the French under Orleans and Marsin at the Battle of Turin, driving them out of Italy before the New Year arrived.

Without Germany or Italy, the men were ordered to approach Spain. King Philip, the fifth and the Duke of Berwick had sent men with news that Madrid was recovered and more men were required immediately. Matthieu grabbed his sword and staff and left for Spain. So while England and Scotland were discussing the Treaty of Union, Matthieu arrived in Spain to help Berwick with another attempt in April. Matthieu helped stop the intruders. One man separated from the fight by shooting Matthieu in the back, chasing him, shouting, "Die stupid man." Matthieu turned around, and the shirt was covered with bullet holes, and the man said, "Why aren't you dead? When will you die?" Matthieu laughed and said, "Why I don't know yet and when I don't know, but I am sorry, but you must not speak a word of this." He hit the man in the temple with the staff and watched him fall to the ground. Matthieu left, and the victory was to the French. A few days later, in England, Queen Anne was named Queen of Great Britain under the agreement of both Scotland and Wales.

Matthieu returned to France with the injured and heard that Prince Eugene was moving from Italy towards France, and Matthieu left again on horseback to face the marching troops. They arrived to cut them off but only a year later, under orders of the Duke of Burgandy, left Marlborough to unite his army with Eugene's, which allowed the allied army to crush the French at the Battle of Oudenarde, and then proceeded to capture Lille on the border.

Matthieu went back to mending the injured when Louis the fourteenth was forced to negotiate; he sent his foreign minister, the Marquis de Torcy, to meet the allied commanders at The Hague. He agreed to surrender Spain and all its territories to the Allies, requesting only that he keeps Naples (in Italy). He was, moreover, prepared to furnish money to help expel Philip the fifth from Spain. The Allies, however, imposed more humiliating conditions; they demanded that Louis use the French army to dethrone his own grandson. Rejecting the offer, Louis chose to continue fighting until the bitter end. He appealed to the people of France. They rallied with new soldiers, money and enthusiasm, giving new life to the French cause. This gave Matthieu a chance to rest, so he left for Paris and hid, only to find the Allies follow for a more serious attempt was launched when Marlborough and Eugene advanced. They clashed with the French under the Duc de Villars at the Battle of Malplaquet. Matthieu heard from the women that the Allies may have defeated the French, but they lost over twenty thousand men, compared with only ten thousand the French lost. By the time September ended in seventeen hundred and nine, Matthieu was long gone and safe from the war.

Four years passed, and Matthieu avoided the violence and bloodshed by working at a factory as their sketch artist. It was May fourth, a year after the treaty was signed, and the first folding umbrellas were debuted. Matthieu worked as their designer for the umbrellas with their patterns. He caught word from a tourist that ten Spanish treasure galleons had sunk off the Florida coast by a hurricane, and the following day a Spanish gold & silver fleet disappeared off St Lucie, Florida. Matthieu was given permission to search for it after saying he had been in those waters before. It was the fifth of July when Matthieu arrived off the coast of the Bahamas and spoke to the indigenous people who had been left alone since Mitchel spoke to Columbus, he asked them about the galleons that vanished north of them, and he was taken to a cave which was full of the missing gold. "We are giving it to the tribes of the islands; this is what we need to live."

"May I take some home to say that this is all that is left,"

"You may take a handful; all the gold is distributed to the people of Arawak, San Salvador, and the people of Espanola."

Matthieu remembered the people he saved on these islands a lifetime ago and smiled as he took the handful and left it on his sailboat. He decided to go to France via Espanola and arrived to see the people thriving, he gave them some supplies as a sign of good faith, and a man led him to a statue carved from solid rock. It was of a man holding a stick. It looked like Matthieu, except the hair was shoulder length. A female voice spoke from a hut, and out stepped a native woman, "You are kind. We show you this statue for it was the first person who showed kindness. He defended my ancestor, the first Leader of the Island. This was a Dominican Queen, and from her came my family line. On behalf of our tribe, we thank you and wish you safe travels. For our blood is connected with the water."

Matthieu arrived back in France after four months of travel, and he told the Spanish that their ships were lost. Only what he brings was found. It was nearing Christmas, and he heard from Englishmen was that the Thames River was frozen. As Christmas drew near, the English pretender to the throne, James the third, lands at Peterhead and Sweden were in Norway.

Matthieu had to find a new job for the New Year, and with King George in England and James Edward Stuart returning to France that February, Matthieu found himself a job in a bakery. He hears that Louis the fifteenth needed a portrait done, and Matthieu saw an opportunity since he painted for the queen of England. Matthieu went over, and King Louis was impressed by his work and agreed. After a month of painting a portrait, he was given a job as a travelling teacher of the arts. Matthieu was given permission to travel to the European countries to teach. He taught for a year in France, and after Henri d'Aguesseau was given his first appointment as chancellor of France, Matthieu left for England since England and France were now on terms with each other after signing the Triple Alliance. In June, he arrived in England and was told he was given the role of painting the stage for George Handel's performance built on the Thames. Matthieu heard about Handel when he was in France from some Italian tourists and arrived at the stage and began to paint when July came a month later, Handel performed Water Music for the King and his guests. Matthieu fixed up the stage for that whole month, and the composition was performed three times. Handel spotted Matthieu one day, painting and whistling, and Handel asked, "Would you mind staying for a few years as my artist? You can paint your perspective during my performances; I really liked what you did with the stage." Handel was nearly thirty-three, and Matthieu looked around forty at the time, making Handel take a liking to him. Matthieu agreed and travelled with Handel for a few years.

Matthieu (Matthew was the spelling by Handel) watched Handel write Acis and Galatea for the first duke of Chandos, the owner of Cannons. He was with him in Dresden after the first Duke of Newcastle, the Lord Chamberlain, requested Handel look for new singers. Matthew was with him as he wrote Oh my dearest, my lovely creature, Brockes Passion, and a few others. He listened to him perform Radamisto, which he did at the King's Theatre while Matthew painted the sets. Matthew returned to France and was told that eighty thousand people had died due to another outburst of the Plague and that the surrounding area was in quarantine. Matthew then travelled to Germany, where he was given permission to listen to Bach perform in Brandenburg. He watched and listened to all six of the performances. When Johann Sebastian Bach played all six, he left after painting a small landscape. He left only to find out that Smallpox, the disease, which killed half the Indians in America over seventy years ago, killed many more. Matthew returned to France after a year in Germany and was at the premiere of 'La Double Inconstance' by Pierre de Marivaux.

Matthew left for England under Machlah Gaston, son of Matthieu, and Handel asked if he had talent and offered money to pay Machlah to paint his Ottone composition. Machlah decided to spend a few years in England. For the next years, Machlah was paid to paint the operas of Handel, all fifteen of them. They were Flavio on the fourteenth of May, then Giulio Cesare on the twentieth of February the next year, then Tamerlano on the last day of October the same year. After that, it was Rodelinda again in February, this time on the thirteenth, then again in March twelfth with Scipione. After that, it was Alessandro on the fifth of May. The next year in twenty-seven was different with the passing of the King and the coronation of his successor. It was June when Handel was asked to write the anthems. Four he wrote, so after Admeto, on the last day of January, Handel wrote Zadok the Priest, which Machlah picked up from the words about Solomon in 1 Kings 1, 'Let Thy Hand Be Strengthened' which Machlah recognised as Psalms eighty-nine verses thirteen and fourteen, the next was 'The King Shall Rejoice' which was from Psalms twenty-one verses one to three and five. Finally, 'My Heart is Inditing' which is from Psalms forty-five verses one, ten and twelve and the Book of Isaiah chapter forty-nine, verse twenty-three. Machlah painted the two together Handel at the Piano holding a stick and King George by his throne holding the staff. The king loved it, and it was named George and George by Gaston. After that, Machlah went back to painting for his operas, the next being Riccardo Primo on the eleventh of November after the coronation in October. The next seven Machlah watched and illustrated were 'Siroe' February the seventeenth, the following year. Then April thirtieth with 'Tolomeo', next was in December with 'Lotario' a whole year later. Then the last few were at the beginning of the next few years with 'Partenope' in February seventeen thirty, 'Poro' in February seventeen thirty-one and finally 'Ezio' and 'Sosarme' both on the fifteenth of the first two months and the last one was 'Orlando' on the twenty-seventh of January seventeen thirty-three.

After travelling back to France, he was called by King Louis himself to be at Versailles. He was anointed as Guard after his family line in the Spanish Succession and was told to be a guard. Machlah agreed and began to use Leonardo's staff to defend the king. He heard from the locals and the royals that a girl aged eleven was reciting plays and could dance like an angel. Machlah then continued to stand guard for eleven years, and it was soon his twelfth when he was told the King asked him to find this famous Madame d'Étiolles. Aged with dust and makeup, Machlah went off to find the salon, where he saw a radiant young girl aged only twenty-four, and he went over and asked, "Are you Jeanne Étiolles, the famous actress, artist, musician, dancer, courtesan?"

"Yes, I am," Jeanne said in her sweet voice.

"I am Machlah, guard of the King, and you are invited to a royal masked ball at the Palace of Versailles on the night of the twenty-fifth to the twenty-sixth of February to celebrate the marriage of the Dauphin Louis de France to the Infanta Maria Teresa of Spain."

On the evening of the ball, Madame d'Etoilles arrived and went to a room of mirrors and waited. She removed the mask. Machlah went with the King and stood at the door when the King walked in and circled her. As the King left, he whispered to Machlah in French that Machlah translated as, "Keep an eye on her. She is young and could be tricky to watch over."

"Oui"

Reinette had turned after the King left, for she was using the mirror to lip read, and said, "So you are my guardian, are you? And what would you do if a man barged in here with a knife."

"I would take the blade for you, 'little queen', and then knock him out cold."

"So, you speak English as well as French, I thought the guards were taught English, and you did your research, knowing the name of my childhood."

"My mother was English." Machlah lied and turned to guard the door as Reinette fixed up her mask and then spoke in Italian halfway, switching to Spanish "Quindi, signore, lei madre era Francese and su padre nació en qué país?" (So, your mother was French, and your father was born in which country?)

Machlah translated the first half and then said "Désolé, je ne parle pas espagnol" (Sorry I do not speak Spanish)

"A guard who speaks English, French and Italian, but not Spanish, yet your father travelled to see if the Spanish gold was lost at sea. I read that in a paper."

"You are intelligent, so are you coming out to dance?"

During the dance, Maclah saw a lady in the corner, she was around thirty and was drinking, but she walked out the hallway and did not come back in.

March came, and the 'little queen' was the king's mistress, and Machlah was hired to paint the room they installed in Versailles directly below his. Machlah was there on the seventh when the official separation between her and her husband was pronounced. Over the next three years, Machlah's hair was proving he was old and when Louis went to him and said, "You have a son, go and fetch him he can take your place, how long will it be to fetch your kin?"

"Give him a year or so. He might not like the idea?"

"Tell him he will be paid well."

"Oui."

Machlah left and two years later arrived back as Mac Gaston. His hair was shorter, his face was cleaner, and his staff was still with him. It was the year seventeen fifty when Mac arrived to take his place. The King was pleased and took him to her room, who knocked on the door and said in French, "Reiny, votre nouvelle garde est là, il est le fils de votre premier garde."

She replied "Louis, je suis occupé avec ce corset, dites-lui de se tenir près de la porte." Mac stood his ground and waited for her to come out. After seven minutes of silence Reinette called out "Garde, peut vous m'aider, le corset sera pas serrer." Mac translated as the corset will not tighten, help me and gulped as he entered the room. Mac entered and saw Reinette was standing with her back to the door, the corset around her waist and the dress around her feet. The strings to the corset were in her hands. Mac walked over and pulled the string tight, and when she gasped, Mac placed his hands in front of her body and slowly moved them up to where the corset met the skin, and his fingers touched her skin and felt her skin tense. She breathed in, and Mac quickly loosened the corset before swiftly walking towards the door, but Reinette spoke in English, saying, "Wait, I might need your help with the dress."

Mac replied, hand on the door, "Young at heart and could be tricky, the King was right about you!"

"Did your father tell you that, for that word tricky was used by Louis himself when I first was put under guard by your father?"

Mac stuttered and opened the door replying, "He did indeed." Mac was halfway out the door when Reinette said in French "Excusez-moi monsieur, mais j'ai besoin encore vos mains"

Mac was stunned. "My hands, you need me to zip up the dress, I assume, for I am married."

"I was married, I am the King's mistress, and I have a daughter named Alexandrine-Jeanne, aged six and could have had two more, but I lost them during labour, so I cannot have the pleasure of what people call romance."

Mac was speechless as he turned around, fixed up the dress, and followed her to the ball. Mac watched her dance and noticed that the Madame spoke to younger women in their mid-twenties and paid them before they left. After the ball, Mac stood by her door that night, around four o'clock. When Reinette knocked on the door and whispered in French "Je ne peux pas dormir, à l'étage de bruit, je savais que je devais ne l'ai pas embauché" Mac went in and saw her in her nighty and then said "You remind me of your father,"

"Same face." Mac laughed and sat down.

Reinette sat on the bed and said, "Tell me about you, what you did for a living?"

"Followed my father with arts; he left when I was only a young to paint for Handel and then guard the King and you, your ladyship."

After talking for half an hour, Mac watched Reinette fall asleep, and then Mac soon dozed off. He woke up to find a piece of clothing over his head. After removing the material, he looked down at the bare feet of Reinette, lifting his head up. Mitchell saw Reinette dressed in nothing but a smile, and then she said, "Strange, you are the first person not to go wide-eyed over my looks. That's new."

"I have seen enough to make up for it and just to take in the beauty of God's people, " Mac half lied. He watched as Reinette went around looking for clothes and muttered.

"Religious man should have known. You are not paying the slightest attention to my looks. You are still staring at my back."

"I saw my wife give birth to my son, so I have seen worse."

Reinette had her shower and returned with a towel, and after Mac helped her again with the corset and dress, Reinette turned to him and said, "As an artist, I have noticed you are an exact copy of your father, except for the long hair."

After that close conversation, Mac went to his quarters and got to work designing a machine. Using rope and the spinning machines used to make clothes, Mac worked on the machine for two years during the shifts he was off. He combined his knowledge of Leonardo and others and created a machine that could tighten a corset. He used a log to test it, and on the twenty-fourth of December, in the year fifty-two, after Franklin discovered electricity with his kite and key, Mac gave the gift to Reinette by taking her to the room after the Christmas Eve ball.

"There's something inside for you." Reinette saw the machine and asked, "What does it do, and how does it work?"

"In the morning, I will show you, but tonight I will guard outside while you change and sleep."

The next morning, Mac showed Reinette how to use the machine by waiting for her to get out of her nighty. When the corset was pulled by hands alone, he used the hooks, tied the string to the wheel, and then told her to pull the lever. She did, and the lever pulled a rope which then turned a wheel which turned another which turned the big wheel with the hooks.

"Better hold onto your bed."

The wheel turned an inch and pulled the strings tightening her corset to make her two inches thinner. Reinette was impressed and, once unattached and dressed, called in the King and the Queen, and they two were impressed after a lady of the house volunteered to be tested. They asked Mac to make more, but Mac spoke, saying, "I made it from designs. What if someone made them instead, for I have to still guard Madame de Pompadour." So, while Mac guarded the Madame, his invention went global in a matter of years, going all around Europe and to America. Mac guarded Reinette until her passing at the age of forty-two. Mac left France after that, saying to the King "I cannot stay to guard a dead body, for I know, from experience, there is no point weeping over them. She is in heaven, and she is happy." Mitchell left and walked into Germany.

Mac arrives in Germany to hear about a boy only aged eight, then remembered the name, as someone who toured France only last year, Wolfgang Mozart. Mac stayed in an inn for a few years. He ran into Benjamin Franklin and asked him about the electricity and showed him his rod during that time. Franklin was impressed by the conductivity of the metal. After that, he moved to Austria, where he saw posters of Mozart going to perform at the age of twelve in Vienna in October. It would be Bastien und Bastienne. Mac went to an art shop, bought some supplies, and began painting the town of Austria. A group of people came up and said, "Can you paint my family?"

"Same," said another woman

"Very well, for a shilling", Mac replied and got to work painting family portraits, the men of Joseph the second came.

"We would like to pay you a crown if you paint the scene of Mozart's opera in the Garden this October. If the parents accept my offer, you will paint for them for as long as you wish." They said.

Mac was thrilled and accepted; that October, Mac painted a piece that the Holy Emperor liked, and the parents agreed for him to stay with them for as long as he wished.

Therefore, as they travelled or stayed at home, Mac was ready to paint the pictures of Mozart. Two years after his first performance, Mozart received the Order of the Golden Spur from Pope Clement. This meant Wolfgang was now the Chivalric Order of the Golden Spur. This was in Rome, and with that, the family was now living in the house of the Archbishop of Salzburg. Mozart already performed for the Archbishop in May, which was called the *'La finta semplice'*. Hence, his next one was in December in Milan, an Italian piece he called *'Mitridate, re di Ponto'* in seventeen-seventy and again in seventy-one, which was called *'Ascanio in Alba'*. After that, Mozart performed for either the Archbishop or another town such as Munich or Vienna. Mac painted for ten years, and after his performance in Vienna in May of eighty-six, Mac was pretending to be twice his age - he used his staff to fake a limp and everything, and his hair was white with paint. Mac retired and headed for Germany. From there, he took a boat to Great Britain and arrived in September to find that England and France had signed a trade agreement, and a fellow named James Watt developed something called a steam engine, a better design than Thomas Savey did in sixteen ninety-eight. America claimed independence from Britain, and King George is now the third. Mac was now Max

Galley and was looking for a job since he had all his money in a box.

Down Under with Phillip, Flinders and Blaxland

Max was walking around Britain to see that all the convicts were being boarded onto boats; Max walked over to a lady at a shop and asked, "Where are these people going?"

"Someplace down under, it was discovered by James Cook. It was spotted earlier, but James Cook thought it is a good place to colonise. So, they are taking the convicts out there to learn to farm and survive."

"Right," Max replied and headed to the docks to see eleven ships waiting to be departed. The passengers boarded. Some were free settlers, ready to explore, others were convicts, and Max counted six hundred male convicts by the chains and two hundred twenty-six females. He then counted approximately one hundred seventy-eight other passengers, including the man at the end; Max walked down to a man who addressed himself as Arthur Phillip. Max turned and said, "Friendship has many loose knots, won't be good in a storm, trust me, I heard of people that drown because of their ship losing sail."

"You know about ships then?" Arthur asked, looking anxious

"I know the ropes, so to speak, had a boat once, sailed the English Channel. Sorry, my name is Max Galley."

"Well, Max, one of our crew is down with the plague, care to join us; it happens that The Friendship is the ship with one less crew."

"Sure, I would be happy; my passengers are convicts, right?"

"No need to worry; they are friendly and excited, sort of. Listen you don't mind; you are only working as an assistant. You follow the orders of Francis Walton, understood?"

"Yes, Captain."

Arthur led Max to Francis and said, "This is Max Galley; he is our last-minute replacement. It is the tenth of May; when can all the knots be ready?"

"Three days tops."

"Get to work, Max!" Max worked on the ropes, and they were off on the thirteenth. Max was on the Friendship, and the people waved as they left. Max went to his bag, pulled out the staff, and tossed it around. A sailor turned up and said, "That is small, is that your baton?"

"Not a baton, a staff!" Max showed it expands and said, "This was a gift from a family friend." And then asked, "What made you agree to this voyage?"

"I want to be one of the first to live a brand-new life, my wife is pregnant, and my father was a drunk. He didn't agree with the marriage, so I agreed to join the First Fleet to start anew, away from him. What about you?"

"Me; was lucky enough to know the ropes and help with loose ends, so to speak."

"Well, off we go."

Max was left on Hygiene and was told to attend the convicts with their baths, using a sponge and a bucket of desalted seawater to bathe the one hundred and four convicts. Max walked in and in a calm voice, spoke on the first night, "Ok, I would like all you women to remove your clothes; they will be washed, for fresh ones are here to use after I bathe you."

One asked, "Got the short straw, did you?"

"Nope, my history leaves me accountable."

"What makes you say that?"

"Before I was on here, I married and left my wife and two kids in Britain."

Max waited for them to remove their clothing, then sponged them down. After that, he went to the men and did the same. After that, Max found a spot to rest and went to sleep. The routine was the same for the next few weeks; Max bathed the convicts at night after maintaining the ropes during the day. They arrived at Santa Cruz at Tenerife in the Canary Islands three weeks from departure to stock up and stretch on dry land, they stayed there for a week, and the convicts were allowed to walk around. Max went to Francis and asked, "How long do you think this voyage will take?" "I say less than a year; we still have to go to Rio de Janeiro and Cape of Good Hope to supplies and livestock."

They left on the tenth and headed into the Atlantic Ocean, Max continued to look after the ropes and the convicts, but as they entered the tropics ten days into the second trip, the weather began to get humid and hot that rats, lice, cock-roche (cockroaches) and bedbugs began to breed and annoy the passengers. Max spoke on the third day and asked for a message to pass onto the other ships to smear the grease in buckets and leave it on deck. That night the buckets were full of rats and cockroaches, and they were tossed overboard. Max was praised for his smart thinking and was in charge of the vermin now as well as the convicts of the Friendship. Another few days passed, and all of Max's ideas worked. He washed all clothes in hot salty water using the fires to boil the water. He also told the people who were being bitten to cover themselves with denatured alcohol or methylated spirits. After washing the clothes, they were soaked in methylated spirits and then dried. All ships were pest-free for the rest of the voyage. The rain kept most passengers below deck, and one night after three days of heavy rain, Max went to bathe the women, opened the hold doors to find the male and female convicts engaging in coitus and said, "Let me know when the male guests have left."

Max told Francis to warn the other captains that the crew and marines are getting bored, and they are passing the time with promiscuity with the ladies both free and captured. Francis acknowledged and asked, "You are married then, but wear no ring, have two kids but agreed to sail to an unknown land; why?"

"I want my kids to know there is more to the world than Great Britain and America."

"Makes sense well better check if the ladies are ready for their wash. The marine's families are already asleep."

Soon after that, the ships arrived at Rio de Janeiro, the day was the fifth of August and the crew were glad to be on dry land. The weather calmed down and the camp was ready by nightfall. Headcount showed that many crew and convicts died due to the conditions. Most were from the Alexander.

They left on the fourth of September after the ships were cleaned and water has taken on board, repairs were made, and Phillip ordered large quantities of food for the fleet. The women convicts' clothing that had become infested with lice were burnt, with the alcohol turning the fires green. They were issued with new clothes made from rice sacks. Even though the convicts remained below deck, Max returned each night to continue his duties and entertain the convicts with a show of fire juggling and using his staff to draw lightning into a bucket of water. Max noticed as he moved from ship to ship that some women were feeling ill and some were sensitive when he washed them around their torso and realised that they were pregnant. They headed east using the westerly winds to push them along towards their next point, halfway along the three thousand seven hundred and seventy-one-kilometre journey a storm picked up from the South Atlantic Ocean breeze and northerly wind from the tropics colliding. The sky turned black and the lightning was their only light. Francis shouted orders for everyone to come in but suddenly a light wind filled with water droplets dampened the flames and their path was darkened. "We are going blind; we have no more matches and I have no idea how to create light."

"That's it!" Max said and shouted over the winds which picked up "LISTEN, CREW, I NEED THREE THINGS TO CREATE LIGHT; ONE, SOME SPIRITS, METHYLATED OR PLAIN ALCOHOL, TWO, A PIECE OF CLOTH PREFERABLY DRY AND THREE, A STICK OR PIECE OF WOOD. OH, I ALSO NEED ONE CLAY POT."

"Are you crazy, how is that going to create light with no matches."

"Matches, who needs matches when you got God providing you the perfect heat source, straight from the heavens to light our way and I will use that heat to burn the spirits."

"How will you do that?"

"Ask the convicts, excuse me, I need to get something from my bag."

As soon as the gear arrived, Max climbed the mast, using the cloth, he soaked in the spirits, that is wrapped around the stick and then tied it to the mast, ensuring that the stick was not too close to the wooden mast. He then hangs from the highest part of the mast, using the staff as a path from the sky to the stick. Francis called for a convict and asked "What is planning to do?"

"Summon lightning" answered the convict and watched as the sky flickered with the light show of the bolts of twenty-seven thousand, seven hundred sixty degrees of heat get closer towards Max. The green flame was seen after the lightning touched the staff, using the clay pot, Max filled the bowl with burning liquid and he climbed down and said "Light, now let's keep moving east."

"What are you, first you agree on short notice, then agree to bathe the convicts, then you remove most of our pests, then you summon lightning with your staff and bring light."

"I am a man of science and of faith; I knew God was helping me along this journey as much as he was helping Paul to Rome, now excuse me I have to relight the lanterns and then sleep."

"A man that willingly would get killed to bring light is a strange man," Francis muttered that night,

They arrived in one piece at Cape of Good Hope on Saturday the thirteenth. It was October and the convicts were tired and some of the passengers were ill and others were pregnant and then some are both. All the convicts were told to help move the livestock and the plants and seeds. Max helped move the animals to the Friendship while the women were moved to The Charlotte. The animals were two bulls, seven cows, one stallion, three mares, forty-four sheep, thirty-two pigs, four goats and a very large quantity of poultry of every kind. Max was told that he could pick another ship to sail in since he wasn't in charge of the animals. Before he could make up his mind John Mason called him over and said, "We have three maybe four women pregnant on my ship, can you care for them, for Francis told me you are a man of science, he had to bury three women from our ship today because they died from internal bleeding from their nose and from their …undercarriage."

"Sure, I would be happy; how many do you have onboard?"

"Maybe one hundred, didn't count."

They left on the second Tuesday of November and continued to sail into the after sailing through rough waters and freak storms, they approached the coast, ships were damaged, and with the HMS Supply, Alexander, Friendship and Scarborough, the fastest ships in the Fleet and carrying most of the male convicts followed, ahead while the others went behind. It was soon January, and the land was in sight. Max watched the horizon as the land became closer. Max had counted a total of near fifty deaths since they left. Max spotted the angel as they were approaching the land, but the girl was gone in one blink. When they arrived in the bay on the twentieth of January to find that area unbearable, Phillip called them to anchor and keep close to the others. The next day Phillip and a party which included John Hunter, departed the Bay in three small boats to explore other bays to the north. Phillip discovered that the land, about 12 kilometres to the north, was an excellent site for a colony with sheltered anchorages, fresh water and fertile soil. Max decided to take a step onto the mainland and noticed people behind trees, dark skin, holding spears and looking worried. Max waded back to the boat and went to check on the convicts, most were up to thirty weeks pregnant, and the kids were bored. So, Max called all the kids onto one boat, The Charlotte where the women he looked after smiled at his return. He juggled fruit and stones, even swords to keep them occupied. After two days, the ships returned and said, "We leave tomorrow for land up north."

The next day two French ships were seen just outside the Bay. This turned out to be a scientific expedition led by Jean-François de La Pérouse. The French were surprised, and when one spoke in French, Max translated, "We had expected to find a thriving colony where they could repair ships and restock supplies, not a newly arrived fleet of convicts considerably more poorly provisioned than themselves." Then they added, "we lost many men near Vanikoro Island", and they stayed in that area to rebuild and stock. However, that night, all eleven ships sneaked off, and by the morning of the twenty-sixth, the fleet arrived in what is known as Port Jackson. The site selected for the anchorage had deep water close to the shore, sheltered, and a small stream is flowing into it. Phillip named it Sydney Cove, after Lord Sydney, the British Home Secretary. {This date is still celebrated as Australia Day, marking the beginnings of the first British settlement.} The British flag was planted and taken formal possession. This was done by Phillip and some officers and marines from Supply, with the remainder of Supply's crew and the convicts observing on board the ship.

The remaining ships of the Fleet did not arrive at Sydney Cove until later that day.

After everyone set up camp, everyone began to settle down and sleep, Max helped nurse the pregnant women, and it wasn't until April when the children were born. Some were born on the ships, for they were impregnated before leaving. Two boys were named Jackson and Sydney for where they were born.

After a while of farming and planting crops, the settlers decided to explore and look around. They didn't go far, for they were still on patrol and were under the careful watch of the marines. Max kept seeing the indigenous people hiding and fleeing from the camp and wondered who they were. After six months of spending nights in the same spot, Max went out to explore, with his staff and his brains, Max started to head off into the great unknown. Phillip had spoken of the natives and how they looked when we first arrived, but since everyone landed, there has been no sign of them. Max went west, and after a week into the unknown, was stopped by mountains; he noticed that there were fewer sights of the Indigenous people. By the time Max completed a full circle and was heading north towards camp, it was nearly January, and he saw the bodies of the Indigenous next to the ashes of their fires and rushed back shouting, "We are killing the natives; send word that the next ship to arrive must bring the vaccination for it."

"That's possible; the ship will leave next season when they head to America and China for more supplies, then the word is sent out for new convicts."

"Wentworth, you're a doctor. Do you think it is possible to vaccinate most of the survivors if I found them?"

"Sure, we already lost thirty men from diseases; we need to be vaccinated as well. I will send word to the Captain, who leaves in two months.

In March the following year, the ship arrived with medicines and more people. The population was now fifteen hundred, and Max and D'Arcy Wentworth gave the Indigenous people a prick in the arm to protect them from the diseases. Wentworth was proud of his work and noticed that Max communicated well with the natives and asked, "My son will be born this year; it might be nice for him to know that the owners of the land are alive."

"How is your wife? She is only twenty weeks, isn't she?"

"Definitely, and she is getting bigger every day."

"That's good news; listen, I think we are finished here. Everyone is done; let's go home or camp,"

Five years later, the population doubled and was now about thirty thousand, with convicts arriving every year and children being born. Some were sent to school on the return ship; others were raised in Australia. A new ship, the HMS Reliance, arrived around September with John Hunter, who had returned to England; the crew included a midshipman called Matthew Flinders and a surgeon named George Bass. Max made friends with them even though he was younger than them in looks; they agreed that he could travel with them if they went beyond Sydney. After they set out in the Tom Thumb in March the following year and returned in April, Flinders and Bass set off on another trip in the Tom Thumb, only until it was the year seventeen ninety-eight when a journey south brought news of a strait separating Van Diemen's Land from New South Wales being highly true, made Flinders and Bass leave on the Norfolk to circumnavigate the island of Van Diemen's Land. Max was called out; as a man in the early forties, Max had his hair clipped short and covered with dust to show 'aging.' They left and headed south until they entered the water; they sailed against it the current and soon ended heading south-west and touching land. Setting anchor, Bass, Flinders, and Max all stepped onto the shore, and while Bass collected plant samples, Max and Flinders met the Indigenous tribes. This continued until they returned to Port Jackson fourteen weeks later with news for the ships to travel straight through the strait on the way in but around on the way out. Later that same year, Matthew discovered that there was land north of Port Jackson; he named the place he landed after the red cliffs.

Max watched as the population increased, and the natives were still hiding even though they came out during the night to hunt wildlife. Flinders arrived back in Port Jackson a few years later, asking for supplies and Max to join him after discovering the whole south coast of the island. Max joined him as he left for Redcliffe in July. As Flinders navigated the ship HMS Investigator, along with the party consisting of a botanist Robert Brown, a botanical artist Ferdinand Bauer and a landscape artist William Westall, Max was carving wood ships of different sizes. Each time botanist Robert Brown rowed to the mainland; Max was there to translate and investigate the indigenous sightings. By the time they arrived back in Sydney on the ninth of June eighteen hundred three, the ship was damaged beyond repair and judged unseaworthy for it was badly leaking. However, even with all this, Flinders managed to return, making him one of the first to circumnavigate the continent completely. He was told that George Bass had left for Tahiti when he inquired. Max farewelled Matthew as he left later that year for England but was surprised by his return, shouting, "Save our crew. They are marooned north on the reef."

***

Max was left alone for a few years growing up, learning the ways of the natives. He learnt to play the didgeridoo and spear fish. People were heading to Van Diemen's Land, and by December eighteen hundred six, the approximate population was nearly eight thousand. William Wentworth was now sixteen but in England and wasn't due back until he was twenty, so Max continued to learn the ways of the Indigenous. It wasn't until another six years, and Max had grown a beard and walked with a fake limp to pretend to be near sixty, when something happened.

"Population is ten thousand, we need more land."

Max heard of a forty-two-year-old man that lived near the mountains who arrived as a free settler in eighteen hundred and five, he started heading west when a voice called out "Max, I am coming with you," Max turned to see young William Wentworth following him, "Take me away from the coast please."

The two arrived to tell Blaxland the problem and he explained "I already did some exploring and found a way to get into the mountains but, have not gone too far alone."

"Lieutenant Lawson has already agreed to come, we will be taking four convicts, five dogs, and four horses laden with provisions, ammunition, and other necessaries," Blaxland continued to explain and then saw Max and said, "What are you doing, you can't come!"

"I am coming, I would like to spend my last few years doing something besides sitting on my bottom and I won't eat much, listen don't talk about me doing anything, I will just translate the natives and speak to them before someone gets hurt."

"Have you heard, that food has been stolen and cooking supplies have been found in the rivers." Lawson said coming over, noticing Wentworth and Max he added "These two coming, that's just dandy, well we better get leaving, fires have been burning land and homes, making people bunk and for some strange reason, I wake up to find dead animals been cooked for meat, such as Emu and Kangaroo, what is going on?"

William replied, "Dad is saying that the natives are getting restless and sick of hiding that they are burning our land."

Max was shocked and said, "When do we leave?"

"Tomorrow, we begin!"

On the eleventh of May the three explorers, with four convicts and Max decided to keep to the ridges instead of endeavouring to find a way through the gullies. They climbed the mountains following the ridges, soon they were up a finger ridge, and it was the twenty-eighth; they climbed down and arrived at a river, which Max said, "Wait a minute, take a look at this." Max pointed with his staff to a rock engraved with the words, 'Where Rivers Meet'. "This is the same river we saw twelve days ago; we could have taken the long road." It was the twenty-ninth of May, and they found themselves on the other side with good grassland before them. After talking to the locals and finding out that a convict named John Wilson had been here seventeen years ago, they left on the first. They followed the rivers back and arrived back at his home five days later. As they returned to Port Jackson, Max heard the yelling of both languages and saw the Europeans pointing guns at the Aboriginals who were holding spears. Asking someone what happened, for the days that they were out, boys and girls went missing for hours on end, coming back covered in blood, and the Aboriginals think that there was bloodshed. Suddenly a shot was fired, and Max saw an Aboriginal being grazed. The sky was dark, and the thunder was rolling in, he directed a lightning bolt towards some dry firewood using his staff. The fire burst, and Max shouted, "WE WERE GONE TO FIND NEW LAND FOR YOU AND WE RETURN TO THIS; THIS ISN'T OUR LAND, SO DON'T

KILL THE OWNERS, AND DO NOT ACCUSE THEM OF VIOLENCE," Max repeated a similar message in the local language and then shouted over the thunder "WE ARE GUESTS, BUT WERE ARE ALSO BROTHERS AND SISTERS, TO PROVE THIS EVERYONE RAISE THEIR RIGHT HAND AND COUNT HOW MANY FINGERS YOU HAVE....FIVE FINGERS AND FIVE TOES, TWO EYES, TWO EARS AND ONE MOUTH AND ONE HEART, WE ARE THE SAME, SKIN COLOUR IS DIFFERENT, NOW LISTEN, IF THERE IS GOING TO BE ANY CONFLICT, COME SEE ME ABOUT IT ON THE CLIFF!"

Lachlan Macquarie stepped forward and said, "What gives you right to say these things?"

"Governor, I have been around since the first Governor stepped foot on the soil; I have seen the works of our diseases on these people. I travelled with Flinders and Bass when they circumnavigated the island. I met the Aboriginals and learned their way of life; I even travelled with these three to find new land, but talking to them, reminds me this is not our land." Max paused and then asked, "How many of you are Irish, how many are convicts, how many of you are free? You all came here for a fresh start, and this is how you do it. I suggest you think before you act; I will be at the cliffs."

"Wait, what about the blood?" asked a concerned adult.

"Let the children that ran into the trees step forward!"

One by one, the children stepped forward, and Max asked politely, "Did you go hunting wild birds with the Aboriginal children."

They nodded, and Max said to the crowd, "If kids can be friendly, why can't adults?"

For the next five years, Max was the middle man for the Aboriginals and the Europeans; with Macquarie still as Governor, Max had his work count out for him. During this time, he wrote on a stone in both languages, and he gave the settlers the idea to build their homes on tree trunks, having a ladder to the ground; that way, floods couldn't affect them and neither could the animals, it also gives the Aboriginals their land as well. He asked the Aboriginals to teach the convict to farm and raise animals, and soon everyone was getting along. It was the year eighteen hundred eighteen, and the number of settlers in Tasmania increased, and the population of white Europeans was now twenty-five thousand. With permission from the Governor, the people made an agreement to live in harmony with the Aboriginals. Max was nearly sixty according to Wentworth and the two children Jackson and Sydney, so Max decided to leave, he took his own ship out in June of the year eighteen twenty after revealing his tablet "These are the rules, they are in both languages, I might not return, but I wish that everyone here will live by them, for each new Governor will swear to follow these rules, I will ask my son, who comes here to make sure that happens."

The stone tablet read for all to see "EVERYONE WILL: SHARE THE LAND, CARE FOR THE LAND, PROTECT THE OCCUPANTS OF THIS LAND, TRUST AND HONOUR EACH OTHER!" Max took the boat The Galley and sailed south to repeat the message to the occupants of Van Diemen's Land and then sailed to Cape of Good Hope and from there to South America before arriving in Hastings on the fifth of February.

Escape the Australian Rush

He tied up the ship and arrived at an inn in Hastings on the night of the fifth, and, as he entered, he heard of a new famous musician, a new Handel or Mozart called Ludwig Beethoven. For the next few nights, he went under the identity of Matthew George. He heard that Beethoven is writing a new composition and will be conducting his opera called Fidelio in November. Matthew George saw what was new in the town since he left with the first fleet over thirty years ago. He walked around and built things from wood, such as toy boats. After a while, he heard that the Royal Academy of Music is established in London. The British Museum is extended and extensively rebuilt during that time to house the steadily expanding collection. He was placed at a school to teach how to carve boats at Rugby School in Warwickshire. He was building a birdhouse when a student was playing Football, everyone was kicking the ball around, and the scores were tied. William Web Ellis recently asked to play and joined in. When the ball arrived at his feet, he picked it up and charged down the field to get closer to the goals. The others did not know what do to, so they charged at him and tackled him to the ground. After a few minutes, he got back up and kicked it to one of his teammates.

Matthew walked over and called out to William, "Nice run, shame that's not the rules to football."

"It is now!" William replied. He shouted to the other kids "Hey, let's play Rugby" and explained the rules. Matthew left and, after the year, headed back to London. He arrived to see Beethoven co-conduct the ninth sympathy. He was in the crowd when he turned to face a woman with golden hair in curls. She smiled, so Matthew asked: "Heard him play before. This is my first one; I only arrived from New Holland two years ago."

"Nope, this is my first time too; shame it will be the last one he ever conducts."

"What do you mean by that?"

"He is deaf; I am saying it will be embarrassing if something happens." The woman walked further into the crowd, and suddenly Ludwig was getting out of time, and the orchestra stopped and went over to him and told him to take a bow. He went red in the face and stormed off. Matthew realised the woman was right but couldn't find her in the leaving crowd.

Matthew changed his clothing the following April, took the staff, then headed out onto the boat and sailed towards New Holland. He arrived on the first of January eighteen twenty-five and found a new Governor. He stepped off and was asked for identification, and Matthew said, "My name is Mason Galley, and my father told me that this place was his life. He hoped that there was no bloodshed since he left, and when he died in bed, he asked me to make sure the law is still his law."

The man said, "Since your father left, a new Governor took Macquarie's place, Thomas Brisbane, and he was really eager for the law, but things haven't been easy. Can you build?"

"Why?"

"For the houses still need to be made, Thomas wants houses on top of houses, two stories for two homes. Listen, why don't I explain."

The porter led Mason towards the trees, and there he saw the construction of houses made of wood and tin. The houses were on four trees above the smaller ones, and the construction was as far as the eye could see. "People are moving up north; some are across the strait, and others will be coming."

That was true, so for the next three years, while Mason was building houses, the settlement in Redcliffe increased. It was not until eighteen twenty-nine when Swan River Colony proclaimed a new Governor for that area, and Mason decided to see James Stirling and ask about the Aboriginals. So, he sailed south to Van Diemen's Land to speak to the people there first. Mason sailed on, and by the time he arrived in Swan River, he calculated the population as seventy thousand. He noticed that there was a statue of wood of a man and a stone tablet. The rules were engraved on the tablet. Mitchell put them in place under the name Max and smiled at the work. He turned and spoke to Governor James and asked about progress, to find out that Darling had sent Major Edmund Lockyer, with troops and 23 convicts, to establish a settlement at King George Sound, but that was changed during November. Sailing north, Mason arrived in Redcliffe the following year to find that they had moved to another location. He sailed back to Port Jackson and, when the new Governor was announced in December, was pleased that the convicts were getting better treated for the next few years.

Mason watched as people arrived to serve their time. He watched the kids of Jackson and Sydney play with the Aboriginal children. Soon it was the year eighteen thirty-two, and the colony Mason visited in Swan River was now renamed Western Australia. Mason caught whispers of escaped convicts fleeing and heading North West. Mason decided to ask the Aboriginals, and he walked for months and arrived at a peaceful town build on rocks and trees. They, too, had a statue of Max, and they welcomed him upon arrival. For the first time, Mason realised that some were

Irish, American, Italian and Greek. They were all living in peace, and for the next eight years, Mason lived with the colony. When they got their border established halfway through it, Mason was smiling. He then left and headed south to explore the coast of Australia and ran into Edward John Eyre in a town called Adelaide, who was planning to explore the coast with an Aboriginal person named Wylie. Mason asked to join, and from there, he and the other three, including John Baxter, crossed Flinders Rangers. They travelled north, and Eyre named a lake "Lake Torrens" they continued north to see how big the lake was and discovered the largest inland lake, "What shall I call it?" Edward asked Mason

"Not after me; Lake Galley sounds weird. Call it Lake Eyre!" and so it was named. They travelled south and arrived five days later at Ceduna. They then travelled west, continuing to follow the coastline, the great cliff to the waters below was an amazing view, but soon they were short of food. John went hunting with two of the Aboriginal People, but when Baxter died from an animal attack and the two fled, Mason signalled help with smoke and was rescued by a French whaling ship out in the Bay, under the command of Captain Rossiter. Eyre named the bay after him, and they continued to Albany. They returned home and arrived months later, making it a new year. Mason left and headed north after spending a week in Adelaide, walking for weeks with little sleep. Mason saw a camel and took a ride towards the rock that seemed to be changing from red to yellow to purple. He arrived on June eighteen, forty-one and met with the locals. They spoke of the rock as Uluru and of the mountains that separated the north and the south. Mason was fascinated, and after climbing to the top the next morning, he arrived at the view of the trees, animals, and people like ants below him. This wasn't like the top of the rock in Van Diemen's Land. He walked back down and continued north. He arrived a month later in the most northern part; he had landed here before, as another person. This time, Mason spoke with the Aboriginals and the people that arrived here. He then travelled back to the Brisbane River colony. By the time he arrived there, people were willingly coming over to settle, and Mason was now pretending to be fifty-six, the staff was a walking stick, and he grew a moustache. Mason lived with the free settlers up north, fishing and swimming.

After a few years, Sir Charles FitzRoy was the governor after Queen Victoria sent him down under. Mason started to walk back to Sydney. The population was staggering to two hundred ninety-three thousand, two hundred forty-nine. Mason realised that his idea of a house on trees worked, and the people were happy living with the view of the water or the treetops. He arrived in the northeast area and caught word of gold being found after camping for a few years. Then people from everyone came to find their fortune. Mason left after finding a pebble size piece of gold and entered the newly named Victoria after the Queen. He arrived at a riverside in the year eighteen fifty-two and began to shift the dirt using his staff. People thought it was crazy for an old man to be looking for gold with a beard and long hair. Until late October, when Mason struck gold, he found a potato-sized nugget, and when people spotted it, they crowded around that area. It was late November when he reached the Bass Strait and looked across to Tasmania. Mason saw an estimated total of ships of one hundred. He sailed across the rough waters and arrived in Tasmania three weeks later in the new year. He arrived in port, walked to the other coast, and saw a statue standing in Hobart. Mason remembered walking past a part of New South Wales where a statue was made of stone that stood in the coordinates of thirty-five degrees south and one hundred forty-nine degrees east. Asking for a large boat, he decided to escape Australia because of the immigrant rush and decided to sail south.

After several hours of sailing, Mason stopped to rest and placed anchor in the middle of nowhere. His mental calendar told him that the day was Friday, the eighteenth of February. He continued to sail and, on the first of March, saw ice. The temperatures were freezing, and animals were everywhere. He landed on the iceberg and decided to make a house of ice for the night. Using slabs of ice, Mason created a home and then went fishing. For three nights, he camped in that spot and then on March fourth, headed south, he followed the stars, and after walking all day, the clock said midnight, and that's when Mason set up camp. The sun rose again around nine o'clock, he continued for another full day, and this time arrived when the sun was still up but just setting. It was eleven p.m. when Mason set up camp and went to bed after midnight when it was still light. On the next hike, he saw that the sun was staying up longer with the more he walked. After a month or two, he finally noticed the sun was up for the whole day. He walked in the sunlight and, at an ice hole, got water and ate any fish that he could catch. It was soon sunset for most hours, and when he calculated the month to be June, the sun was no longer in the sky. He noticed the stars when he gazed at the sky and noticed they were different. For the next few days of darkness, he created fire from matches (he had supplies from the ship) and walked for a whole month. And noticed the stars change the directions he went, the compass also changed, and he realised he was exactly south. He was on the bottom of the earth.

Mason waited until the sun began to rise after another month (August twentieth) before he walked back to the ship. He arrived a few months later, and the sun was again high in the sky. He sailed north towards the island, which he thought was Van Diemen's Land, but with rough waters and high winds, he arrived on the shoreline with people that didn't look like Aboriginals, and they spoke another language. When he tried to explain, suddenly a man spoke and said, "And you are?"

"Mason Galley the second"

"Well, Mason, I am John Smit, and you look like you sailed from our cousin island Van Diemen's Land."

"It's a state, not an island, and in some sense, yes, I did. I need to stock up supplies for my journey, and I arrived here by mistake."

"This is New Zealand, and we just had our first election. Why don't we introduce you to Governor Sir George Grey and our brothers, the Māori."

"Māori, are they the indigenous people of this land?"

"Yep, and after Eyre spoke of how Max Galley convinced the Europeans to behave and be nice, we decided to do the same."

Mason met with the people of New Zealand, and after being given fresh clothes (his were soaked from the ice, he asked for his undershirt to be dried, and George Grey commented on the pattern "That looks like a map of some sorts, strange design!"

"I made it to remind me of something, it was sewn by hand, and it is the only item of clothing I keep."

"How long will you stay here?"

"Maybe until March next year, I will be taking my ship back too"

"Strange name for the ship, the HMS Splinter"

"It was a boat my size", and Mason went to sleep.

When March approached, and George Grey was no longer governor, Mason sailed south again with a compass, a year supply of food and clothes, and his watch and staff. The water got rough, and the Splinter began to sink after a month on the water. He, however, arrived at the iceberg, and the ship was going down. He had enough time to place everything onto the iceberg and collect driftwood. He found his camp and carried his supplies into the ice house. He woke up the next morning to see no sun and realised it was the dark hours. He spent the next three months eating and sleeping, and when it was twilight, he created a sled and dragged the supplies to his next camp. He reached the south pole by the end of the year, and it was daylight again. He pulled out the potato-size piece of gold and decided to bury it in the ice. Using his spear and some picks created a hole and placed the gold in a tin can. He wrapped it in cloth and buried it one hundred meters under the ice. He then looked around, and after camping for another month, it was the year eighteen fifty-five. He walked until the compass told him he was heading northwest. Days walking in sunlight, he spotted penguins and whales and birds. He arrived after months of walking at a place that was perfect to camp and built another home. He then walked again until the sun did not appear over the horizon, he was cold but alive, and when the stars came on the fourth night of pure darkness, he prayed, "Lord, you are Creator of all; I have seen the people, that do not resemble us, I saw black and yellow, I know Father that you are loving and what I did long ago was the right thing to do, and I understand that I am here to make a difference." He looked at the necklace he had and said, "My parents are ash and bone, my family is dead, but you are my eternal father, and I will not let you down."

It was soon September, and twilight was brighter, so he continued to walk, and soon he arrived at the coast of the iceberg. It was a big drop, so he found a place to walk down. He arrived on a shallow coast and wondered how to get off the iceberg. Then he spotted his blanket, staff and the ropes he had left. He knew he was nearly out of supplies and decided to make or break a boat from ice and supplies. He stood the staff upright in the ice and tied the blankets to make a sail. He then pulled together rope and other supplies and made a rudder and oars from wood and then paddled until he was tired, and then the wind picked up, and he sailed north. After months of slow sailing, he spotted land and arrived at a familiar port. The ice was melting, and soon he was floating on his suitcase to the wooden dock. He carried himself to the mainland and realised it was Port Elizabeth, seven hundred eighty kilometres west of Cape Good Hope. He decided to walk to Europe, which bordered Africa, so he walked into the heart of Africa. Mason walked through the jungle for months, seeing the elephants, hippopotamuses, rhinoceroses, and wild cats. The days he was injured, and the nights he healed. He walked without a shirt for most of the trip. After nearly two years of walking, he arrived to find a tribe of people looking down after he fainted from exhaustion and lack of food. They spoke to him in a foreign language, and after a while, he understood they were talking about him. He sat up and said, "Hungry need food!" and pointed to his mouth. Suddenly a man spoke in their language, and everyone rushed away; the man spoke in English, "Welcome, brother, I am Sechele."

"My name is M; I have lived for so long I don't know my name,"

"Old, you look younger than me."

"Appearance can lie; I am old, older than you and older than your father, to be honest."

"Then I will call you Maalik, meaning experience. You are wise beyond your years."

"How come you speak English?"

"Met a fellow white skin, who spoke English, eleven years back in eighteen forty-seven, named David Livingstone, who taught me about God."

"A fellow man of faith, like myself, well, I have been walking for a year and a half. Can I rest here for some time?"

"Rest until you can walk again. We will give you food and water as well as a fire to keep you warm at night."

It wasn't until January in the eighteen fifty-nine that Maalik took his staff and continued to walk; he was given food and water and a coat from a lion and directions. Maalik walked onwards. He arrived in Bulawayo on February first of the following year and met with a tribe of Indigenous people, he had run out of food, but they gave him berries and wild game. He stayed for a night and continued to walk the following week. He arrived in Lusaka in Zambia on Tuesday the fourteenth of May the following year and spent a week meeting the people. He explained his reason for walking, and they laughed and led him to a bird that was tied to a tree. It looked like an emu, but it was black and pink. He climbed on it and was told it was an Ostrich and that it was fast. He arrived in Sudan three days later. He stocked up and ran on the fast bird to Egypt on Saturday the twenty-fifth of May. He arrived Sunday around midnight. He found a place to camp, and he went looking for a boat to take him to Europe. He sold his Ostrich for money and bought a ticket on a carrier boat to Greece. He left on Monday around eleven-thirty and arrived on Thursday around seven-thirty.

When Maalik stepped off the boat on the dock of Piraeus in Greece that morning, the nimbus clouds gathered as the people did. They all began to stare at him; he looked around and noticed that he had a bare chest and wore fur. He must have looked strange. They all started to chant "Ηρακλή, έχει επιστρέψει." If Mitchell's Greek was correct, he translated to, "Heracles, he has returned."
Maalik realised they thought he was Heracles, so he shouted in Greek. "I am not Heracles!" but as he raised the staff, the switch flicked, and it extended and the lightning shot from the sky and brightened up the town. The people were in

shock, and after he explained repeatedly, someone stepped forward. "My name is Abderus, and I am the representative of this town. May we know your name?"

"My name is Maalik Grain, I came from Africa to travel to France, and I am not Hercules!"

"Yet you wear lion fur and can summon lightning."

"A tribe in Africa gave me the coat. This stick I hold here is a work of science!"

"Well, then come and enter the tavern and talk of this science."

Maalik entered the tavern but did not drink. He asked for milk and then turned to Abderus.

"My family has been travelling the world for centuries, making homes here and there, this staff was made in Italy, and after many centuries I am returning to my hometown in France" Mitchell told half the truth.

"Have you ever been there?"

"No, I haven't seen France", Mitchell lied as he was given his drink. "I have only heard about it from stories my parents told me. How long do you think it would take to get to the northern part of Greece that is closer to France, I believe."

"Well, first let us show you the sites, we walk to Athens and then from there you can have a horse to ride to the sites and then we will find you a boat. Besides, no boats leave for France this time of year."

Maalik walked to Athens and learnt their way of life. He learned to play Greek sports, played their games, and read and write in Greek. After three months, he was given a horse and rode north to see Mount Olympus. Riding for a fortnight on the horse, he arrived in Lamia and from there, after spending the night, he left on Monday the sixteenth of September and rode the horse north to Larissa. The journey took ten days. He then spent the weekend there and left on the last day of September and headed to the Mountain. That took him five days, and when he arrived, Maalik knew he had to climb it. After three weeks of nonstop climbing, he arrived at the top, and then he climbed down and continued his journey to the west coast. He arrived two weeks later to find that the boats won't be leaving until next year. He caught wind that a boat would be leaving Piraeus at Hercules Port (the place near where he stepped off) in two months. He rode as fast as he could on the horse to make it. He arrived a month later with rest for nights; the date was December sixteenth, and the boat was due to leave on January the fifteenth. In the new year, he took the boat making it eighteen sixty-two and arrived on the twentieth of January in Cannes, France.

Adventures of Gold and Jules

January: Mitchell left a hotel as Midas Gold, went to the shops, and saw a needed way to reach Paris. Midas saw two broken spinning wheels thrown out and remembered the wagons he saw. He went to work. Midas put together a land vehicle that would travel downhill and up using iron scraps. He hopped on and then began to test it. It was dark by the time he finished it. The next morning Midas rode the vehicle along the dirt paths to Paris. He rode left to the paths of St John, he then turned on Antibes Street, and from there, his journey began, with left turns and right turns. Midas rode the bi-wheeled vehicle all day and all night. Midas arrived in Roanne, and he found an inn to sleep in for the night. He was unaware that people were looking strangely at this wheeled device or speaking rapidly in French about a man called Jules Verne, who wrote plays and a book called "The 1857 Salon"; they spoke about him trying to find inspiration for his next big thing. Midas went to sleep that night and thought about how much Paris has changed since he was here in the eighteenth century over one hundred years ago. He dreamt of Reinette and then of George and all the other people he met. The dream changed, and it appeared to be the girl with sunshine blonde hair. She was walking around repeatedly muttering, "Nope, this is my first time too. Shame it will be the last one he ever conducts." Midas left soon after he woke up and headed towards Paris, people stared at his bike, and after a day and a half without rest, Midas arrived in Paris. On the evening of the very next day, Midas saw what once was a palace was now opened for the wealthy. Midas had money and went in to explore, and after a while of seeing portraits and ignoring the artwork of Leonardo, he went to an inn and went to sleep. Midas left for Nantes after hearing about Jules Verne during breakfast; around noon, he left for the hometown of this Jules, and his ride was falling apart. After a few hours of riding on a broken bike, the wheels broke after a day of riding from Paris, and Midas was left stranded by the side of the road. Midas woke up to see a horse-drawn cart pull over. A man stepped out and walked over, "What are you doing laying on the side of the road? You know thieves can steal from you out here?"

"I lost my ride and fell asleep; I haven't got any way to reach Nantes. I am looking for someone that might like what I have to say."

"Well, hop in, and we shall head there; I am on my way there. My wife and first-born son are waiting. I just went to Paris to see if someone would listen to me."

They hopped aboard, and both rode the carriage to Nantes. On the ride, Midas introduced himself and told the stranger about his trip walking through Africa and meeting the people and the fact that the Greeks thought he was Hercules. He then finished by explaining the fact that he would love to explore the world by air. They arrived in Nantes, and the man stepped out and said, "Now, who did you want to see?"

"Jules Verne."

"Well, you are looking at him, I am Jules Gabriel Verne, and I would love to have you as part of my team for research. I have just met this fabulous man by the name of Pierre-Jules Hetzel, and if I finish this book before the year's end, I can have it published."

"What's the matter?"

"I cannot work out the times I have the information but not the times."

"What you would like me to do?"

"If you can travel the path I give to you, according to my notes and friend's advice, you can tell me how long it takes. I will organise a ride for you when I get to my house."

Midas left with Jules, and after Jules organised a ship to leave the Thames on the twenty-first, Midas will be off to Zanzibar. Midas went to sleep on the lounge and said to himself, "This is going to be a fun trip."

February: Midas continued to live with Jules and his family and tell tales of his ancestors, which were his past lives; he showed them Leonardo's staff and explained the process of flying. During this time, Jules calculated the amount of energy it would take for their makeshift balloon of parachutes and a large hand-woven basket to make it safely across Africa. Midas promised he would record the dates and times, and then, on the night of the twenty-first, Midas prayed to the Lord. "Lord, be with me on this journey, help me travel in the air, be with me as I cross Africa." On the twenty-third, Midas rowed out the boat that was waiting, the crew was only six, and they had supplies for a month on water. Midas had a journal given to him by Jules and a dove to send him information if they needed to. Midas waved as the ship left the waters and sailed towards the Canary Islands. They sailed, and soon, it was March.

March: Midas was going over calculations and procedures once he stepped off the ship and landed in Tanzania, he was aware of the animals, and now he was aware of the dangers of falling. He prayed each night, and after twenty-six days at sea, they saw land. It was the coast of South Africa, the resting point of the first fleet. Midas thanked the Lord, and they landed on the Cape City and stocked up. They set up camp, before resting; after eighteen days on dry land, Midas awoke one morning to get ready to continue. The first two pages were full of notes, and they continued to sail and head towards the east coast.

April: Midas sailed with the crew northwards and onwards towards the coast of Tanzania. It was early morning when they left, and after adding an hour to the clock, they soon reached three o'clock post meridiem time, and it was getting later. Midas told stories to the crew about the animals in Africa, and after a few hours of sailing, it was nightfall. Midas awoke after seven nights to see they had passed Madagascar and were approaching the coast and the city of Zanzibar. On the fifteenth, Midas tied up the ship and, with some help from the crew, set out to set up the large balloon. They arrived earlier than expected, so Midas wrote in the journal, "Arrived eleven o'clock, instead of predicted three o'clock." Midas then went to find the chief of the people of Tanzania. However, the people did not like the idea of Midas heading into the sky and protested. They believed Midas, a man of faith and religion, should not try to reach God. Midas studied their language on the boat said "Mimi si kufikia Mungu, nami kufikia upande mwingine wa Afrika, mimi si hata kupita mawingu." Which meant, "I will not reach God, I will reach the other side of Africa, I will not even pass the clouds."

They were shocked and then Midas said "Nilikutana na watu wengine wa nchi yako, i kutembea Afrika tu miaka michache iliyopita." Meaning "I met with others from your country. I walked Africa only a few years ago." They spoke amongst themselves, and when they saw the lion coat said all at once, "Kuondoka kwa haraka kama unaweza, basi hatuwezi kukuumiza." In other words, "leave soon, then we cannot hurt you. Midas thanked them and then went back to where the ship had set up the balloon. They camped that night with talk of the adventures Midas would have. After days of organising the furnace with help from James Watt, it was soon morning of Good Friday. It was nine in the morning when the steam filled the balloon, and the crew waved goodbye with a message of seeing him on the other side. They will be waiting to pick Midas up on the other side of Africa. The dove will find them with his location on a note. Midas was sitting on the balloon named after the balloon in Jules's manuscript; the Victoria was sailing southwest and at the height of twenty-five hundred feet. Two hours later, Midas reached the coast of Africa, and from the Victoria, he could see the ant size animals stalking and moving, following their daily routine. From there, he lowered the balloon after going higher to cross the strait achieving three hundred feet of altitude heading south. He passed a small village that Jules called Kaole. Midas was surprised by how quickly he was travelling. And soon, he was over the Uzaramo District, which was still south of the Nguru Mountains. After gaining speed and going twelve miles, he crossed villages to see them rant and rave. It was soon late, and Midas saw a mountain. Going over it, Midas soon was on the other side.

Midas set off after a night on the other side of the mountain; he continued going west and soon arrived at the longitude of thirty-six east. He then sailed over a lake, writing in his journal that he had something to drink and watching the animals come to the lake like ants to a drop of water. Midas checked his altitude and found it six hundred feet, and he was heading northeast instead of west. He was heading straight for the Rubeho Mountains, and once inside it, he was following the channel of wind. He was soon westbound and running out of water. He saw a lake in the distance and, after a while, tied off and went to collect some water. He walked for an hour and soon saw something rare. A Bluebuck or a blue antelope hiding in a cave near the water source. Midas drew a picture and then sent the dove with news to Jules. He walked back, continued to float, and let the wind carry him to his destination. Around seven o'clock, Midas was over a basin, and he stopped for the night around nine. Midas arrived at Kazeh and headed northwards. Midas continued to jot down the journey in the book and, after a few days, found himself at thirty-two degrees forty minutes east longitude and four degrees seventeen minutes latitude, somewhere in South Sudan. He found a river that he guessed was what Jules was looking for and followed it back to the equator, and ended up at a lake in Uganda.

Midas followed the rivers, found the Nile, and sent the dove that returned with information for Jules. He then turned on and continued to float west. It has been days since Midas left the island with only a journal and the sun to keep track of time.

May: Long days of wind, rain and sun, and on Thursday of the first of May, the scorching sun made no effort on the flawless skin of Midas. His body recovered from the burns and was quick to warm up during the cold at night. With repeated hours of the same pattern, Midas looked over and saw the Sahara Desert and recorded the desert's location in the journal. He continued to float over the Sahara for the next few days, and soon his throat was parched. Then he spotted an oasis surrounded by trees. Midas drank with the animals after trying the balloon to a tall tree and, at nightfall, set off again. However, he was running out of wood, and the trees were only enough for a few more hours. The water he had wasn't enough, and by Saturday, he was low on supplies.

After another day, he ran out of wood and began to walk after letting the balloon drift and be carried by the wind a few miles across. Midas walked until he spotted something ahead, some dead wood. He carried the wood and began to float again, and after another day in the air, he found another oasis, this time with plenty of water, and after his eyes played tricks on him, he landed and walked towards the water. Lions attacked the bare chest of Midas as he walked towards the clear liquid. Midas drank as his body healed and, after near four days without water, was glad to be leaving on the seventh with wet lips. He wrote the coordinates down for Jules "fifteen degrees forty-three minutes east longitude, and eight degrees thirty-two minutes north latitude." He continued on, and after days of seeing some plants and animals, he soon saw people and civilisation. He floated over and continued to write down the information for Jules to make on the facts. Midas was away from people by May eleventh and again floating over the desert. He dreamt during the nights of a girl walking around Africa, but he woke up every time he tried to speak to her. Noon on the twelfth, Midas realised he had ten days left to go before he should reach the end of this journey. He sent word asking where the boat was located and found out it was passed Good Hope and heading up towards the west coast and will be waiting until they can spot the balloon. Ten days later, Midas crossed Africa and reached the ocean. He saw the blue in the distance and lowered the balloon. After hours of flying, he saw where the trees and the water met and landed the balloon. He had a journal full of facts and figures, and after hours of emptying the balloon and putting it on the ship, Midas told the crew, "Home, please; I can't wait for a nice bed and breakfast!"

June: Midas arrived Wednesday the first of June and handed the journal to Jules, who was thrilled and said, "Thank you." Midas left with Jules and found an Inn. They drank, and Midas watched as the others swallowed the alcohol and celebrated the journey. Midas asked Jules what was going to happen now, and Jules replied: "I will finish the book and then find you out for my next one. I shall start next week. First, we celebrate."

Midas stayed in this inn for the next few months, and when the book was published, Midas was given the first official copy; Midas turned to Jules and asked, "What is your next book about?"

"I am working on a few. Have you ever been to Iceland?"

"I can't say that I have, but my ancestors have." Midas lied, his mind going back to the years sitting on the coast, "Why do you ask?"

"For my next book starts off in a mountain called Snæfellsjökull that is one hundred ninety-four kilometres from the capital, Reykjavik."

"Sure, I will travel to Snæfells and see what it is like. When shall I leave?"

"Second day of the month…. this summer."

"So, June eighteen sixty-three is the month?"

"That is correct!" Jules replied and started giving him a list of supplies. Midas knew how to climb mountains and thought this would be easy. It soon was the twenty-first of June, and Midas left at eight in the morning on a boat heading towards Reykjavik to begin his way to Mount Snæfellsjökull. After five days in the sea, Midas arrived to restock and find a horse to ride. Two days later, it was the twenty-ninth of June and Midas arrived at the mountain base. It was dawn, and Midas began to climb. Five hours later, Midas reached the top of the Mountain and from there, he began to find any caves in the rocks that were at the top. Using the staff, he scaled the last rocky parts of the mountain. When the clouds gathered, static began to turn the sky grey, the rain began to fall, the rocks began to get wet, and Midas used his staff to continue to get a grip when the lightning began to strike around him. Midas bolted when he saw a cave. As he ran, the staff collapsed and was placed in the leather satchel he carried.

Jumping into the cave, the lightning sent rocks to fill in the last rays of sunshine. Midas was trapped. Midas gathered his thoughts as he counted his supplies and realised he had enough food for three days. He saw a tunnel and followed it down deeper into the mountain. He went deeper and deeper, and after a few hours, he arrived at a few old lava tunnels and decided to take one that he thought would lead up. Still, after a few more miles, he realised he was going down instead of up. Suddenly he tumbled and landed on what he saw as many shining stones. He went over and found diamonds, emeralds and what appeared to be other precious stones that people try to collect. Midas took one or two of each when suddenly he heard the ground creak beneath him. Midas looked down and saw that he was standing on shale, and suddenly, Midas fell; as he fell, he struck his head and went unconscious.

Midas woke up and found himself at the bottom of the water source, he was wet and cold, and everything was floating around him. He swam to a shore and looked up at the space above. Suddenly he saw birds that were glowing. They were luminescent birds that he saw in paintings and dreams. They were Cyanis rosopteryx but different. He walked towards a gap in the rock walls and suddenly saw a huge cavern filled with light and plants. He walked deeper into the new land

and saw what looked like a forest of gigantic mushrooms, at least forty feet high. Midas continued to walk, fascinated by what he saw. Unaware, Midas's brain was hit hard, and he lacked oxygen, which put his body into a stable coma.

Midas was on the shores of Iceland, eyes closed and dreaming the whole scenario. For days Midas lay in the coma, and for days, Midas laid motionlessly on the shores of Iceland. Midas wandered endlessly in the forest of flowerless plants and mushrooms for days. It was only after a month of walking and a month of sleeping was when Midas was found in real life. During this time, Midas was at the shores of a central sea. Midas built a raft of wood, blankets, leaves and ropes used during the hike. After a few hours of building, Midas was ready to sail. In real life, Midas was taken aboard a boat heading south towards Italy. Soon Midas was sailing the thermal winds on the ocean tides. He was on the sea for twelve days, and for twelve days, the ship carried Midas to Italy. When the ship hit rough seas, Midas dreamt of giant monsters rocking the waters around the boat during the journey. Midas arrived on the other side and followed the deserted rocky shores to a geyser on the other side. From there, Midas blew a hole and travelled upwards after letting water out into the lava below. As he rode upwards towards the sky, his body was given a jumpstart, and Midas woke up in Sicily. It has been two months since he arrived in Iceland. He asked what happened, and when he was found by the crew that dropped him off, Jules was waiting. Midas told Jules about his dream, and Jules said, "That will make the book ten times better."

For the next few years, Midas helped Jules by being his muse, and it wasn't until September eighteen-sixty-seven that Jules asked Midas to come with him to London. However, Jules told Midas that he would arrive in ten months after following a path he had written for his next novel. Midas was given the instructions to head to Japan or near Japan and follow the route of his next character, Captain Nemo. Midas read the instructions and agreed on one condition. "You come the minute the dove arrives with orders to pick me up, I may be a survivor, but I am not going without any life support."

Jules agreed, and Midas was taken on a ship called the Lincoln. Midas and a crew of fifteen set sail to where the ship would arrive in Japan approximately in fifty days, they stopped at Good Hope and stocked up, and from there, they sailed onwards to Japan. Midas looked at the small boat on the ship and saw the oars, the sail, and the storage. The ship was enough for ten people but would only carry one. Midas noticed chains and metal and remembered the vehicle he made with two wheels. He began to weld and after twenty days on the sea, Midas created a gear powered blade that he tested and pushed him faster along the water. The captain was impressed and laughed when he spoke of Jules Verne "Apparently, the vehicle this Captain Nemo would take goes underwater and powered by energy from an atom." Midas pondered over the idea as they arrived in Japan. They were left at the coordinates of thirty-one degrees fifteen minutes north latitude and one hundred thirty-six degrees forty-two minutes east longitude. Midas pulled the chain and began the journey following the course given by Jules.

November: Midas arrived at the coordinates 31 degrees 15 minutes north latitude and 136 degrees 42 minutes east longitude. He sailed for twelve days later at 32 degrees 40 minutes north latitude, 157 degrees 50 minutes west longitude, where he saw a tiny island from an extinct volcano. He dove for seaweed and continued onwards. He crossed the Tropic of Cancer ten days later and, in the distance, saw Hawaii. Midas crossed the Equator on the first of December.

January: Christmas and New Year passed, and Midas celebrated on the boat. He prayed to the Lord for a safe journey. However, on the fourth, he was grounded. He walked on the shore the next day and was sailing through the strait at two-forty in the afternoon. Midas crossed the Equator again by January twenty-sixth and headed north towards India; two days later, Midas dove for pearls and was back sailing within three hours. Sailing into the Arabian Sea, then the Persian Gulf and finally the Red Sea, he reached the end of the Red Sea, and before he touched the Suez Canal, he went underwater and came back up in the Mediterranean. Midas saw he was out of supplies and sent a dove requesting new supplies. He was only carrying his satchel and staff. Leaving the Mediterranean behind, Midas continued on. He passed Spain and realised he still had months before meeting with Jules in London. Going South, Midas headed into the Atlantic, and after a few days, he reached a spot in the middle of nowhere. He was given supplies from a Spanish ship once he left the Mediterranean near Canary Island. His coordinates were sixteen degrees seven minutes West Longitude, thirty-three degrees twenty-two minutes North Latitude. Using the gear he was given by the Spanish, he dove into the ocean and about one hundred kilometres under the surface, he spotted a city. It was like an island of volcanic rock. The base was still in one piece, held down by the marble ruins. Buildings, houses with no roofs made from marble or rock, the style was from the early times to Midas it was like looking at the ruined city of Pompeii which he visited while in Italy, a thousand years ago. Many people believed it was a continent between America and Europe, but Midas believed God had something different in mind when he created Earth and Sea when He made the universe. This looked like an ancient city dating back eighteen hundred years or more. It looked like a city that had sunk and moved miles away from its original destination. Running out of air, Midas returned to the surface and continued on.

March: Midas sailed south until after fourteen days into March, Midas saw familiar ice. It was the Antarctica coastline. Midas was there but further along, remembering the days on ice with a chunk of gold, it was only a few decades ago when Midas was walking near here. After tying the boat to an iceberg, he arrived at the coastline and climbed the wall and walked to the edge of the downhill slope. He made a shield of metal from scrapes. It was basically a large disk, and with a push of his staff was riding the metal down the slope towards the centre. He arrived at his gold in five full days without eating anything. He went so fast that the ice was melting with his body heat. Turning around, Midas scaled the ice back to his boat, five months had passed, and Midas was still no closer to London.

April: It took eight days to return to the boat and two days to reach South America. By the eleventh, Midas reached the Amazon River's mouth. He continued to sail north with the winds aiding him. He powered on until it was the twentieth, and Midas sailed past the islands he discovered with Columbus. He did not wish to invade after giving them freedom, so he sailed onwards.

May: Sailing through storms, Midas passed the American coast with only seeing darkness, the dove had trouble reaching London, and when the storm was over, London was on the horizon.

June and July: Midas sailed past London and north to Norway for two months, where he finally landed. Midas was put on the first boat to England, where he arrived on the west coast four days later. He rode horseback to London. While Jules went his way. Midas searched for the famous Charles Dickens that he heard from in France and remembered a line William said to him when he saw his house. "What the dickens!" Midas found Charles when he returned from America in ill health. Midas decided only to give a letter, and then he walked away and returned to Thamesport to meet with Jules, who was delighted with the results.

After another two years since the book was published and Midas had a copy, Jules asked Midas if he wanted to travel the globe in less than four months. Midas had gems, pearls, and his staff in his satchel and agreed on one condition. "I have money this time, and I can have days with rest."

"Certainly!" Jules replied and gave him the instructions. It was basically a list of towns he had to get a passport from before travelling onwards. Midas sighed and agreed to do this. Looking again at the itinerary, Midas saw his first place was in London, so with a suitcase of clothes, his undershirt, his staff, the satchel and enough money for six months, Midas had currency from all the trips he was paid by the publisher. Midas went to London by boat to take him to France again at a specific time. Midas was to start on Thursday, the second of May, eighteen seventy-two and arrive back on Sunday, the twenty-first of July. Midas left Amiens and arrived at Boulogne-Sur-Mer after eight hours on a penny-farthing. Next, he crossed the channel and arrived in London after half a day on the water. The boat left and would wait for him at his next destination. Midas caught a train to Dover at quarter to nine; he then boarded a boat to Calais, which took him only three hours. Midas caught a train to Paris, which he arrived on the third of May around seven twenty, then from there he travelled to the border of Italy at Turin and then from there to Brindisi. He made it in with an hour to spare, for the steamer, which left at five in the afternoon and going at eleven and a half knots, arrived in

Suez in three days eighteen hours. In Suez, Midas wrote down what he had done "Left London, Thursday, May 2nd, at 8.45 p.m. Reached Paris, Friday, May 3rd, at 7.20 a.m. Left Paris, Friday, at 8.40 a.m. Reached Turin by Mont Cenis, Saturday, May 4th, at 6.35 a.m. Left Turin, Saturday, at 7.20 a.m. Arrived at Brindisi, Saturday, October 5th, at 4 p.m." From Suez, he arrived in Bombay early due to good weather, the engineer being a fan of Jules and accepting the challenge and the agreement of money. It was the twentieth, and the train was to leave precisely at eight at night. After a day having Indian food, Midas boarded the Great Indian Peninsula Railway, in which Midas arrived at Berhampur in sixteen and a half hours. Midas used the money to buy some clothes since he was repeating the same fashion; he bought traditional Indian clothing, a hat, shoes and a traditional banyan. Getting back on the train, he continued on and soon arrived the next day around eight o'clock, nowhere near his destination, Midas asked the driver what was wrong and he replied, "The rail has to be repaired; we stop here."

"How am I going to reach the station to arrive at Calcutta?"

"Try an elephant!"

Midas found an elephant and took the journey on the four legs of the elephant, and after a few hours, he ran into trouble. A couple of people were attacking a young girl. Since it was the twenty-third of May and Midas had two days to reach his destination, he decided to help. Midas pulled out his staff after changing clothes, and he saw the storm that was gathering that night which gave him an idea. He placed the staff down and then stood in front, and as the lightning was attracted by metal, Midas shouted, "I am the Mal, a messenger of God. LEAVE THAT GIRL ALONE!"

The men stopped attacking the girl and ran away. Midas took the girl's hand, and they rode all the way to Allahabad. Caught the train to Calcutta, the steamer would leave at noon on the twenty-fifth of May. The girl asked to be taken to China for her parents were there. The two arrived at seven, and with five hours to spare, Midas bought breakfast and asked the girl to join him. The girl was named Aouda Mai Ling. She explained that she was promised to a man in India but was tricked into slavery; she escaped and was chased by the three men. After five days, they were approaching Singapore, and on the last day of May, he arrived in Singapore. At eleven o'clock, the Rangoon rode out of Singapore harbour.

June and July: They arrived on the sixth a day late in Hong Kong, and from there, he left for Yokohama but missed the steamer by taking Aouda home and with four days to make it to Shanghai to catch up, Midas left on another boat.

Jules planned this, but when Jules got word of it, he was happy to change the storyline to make it fit. He arrived on the fourteenth and headed towards San Francisco; he arrived on the third of July. He had eleven hours before the train, and when he boarded at six o'clock and after fifteen hours of travel, Midas entered the State of Nevada through the Carson Valley. They had a breakfast break at Reno, and the rest of the trip had interruptions that followed. From buffaloes to American Indians but after talking to them and straightening things out, Midas soon arrived in New York forty-five minutes late for his boat to London. He arrived at quarter past eleven on the eleventh, and he had only ten days to arrive back at London. He had not looked at his watch, which would have told him the time in London. Instead, he was looking at the clock at the dock. He found a boat that left at nine and boarded it. He left and was heading across the Atlantic Ocean. The boat was heading to France, but after a day of stakes, Midas explained the reason to be in Liverpool, and the captain agreed on the condition to give him the majority of the money he had to get there.

Midas was nearly out of banknotes on the sixteenth, with five days to go. He had the jewels, but that wasn't important. The boat was heading towards Liverpool but was running out of steam. The coal was short for this trip. By the eighteenth, they were nearly empty and with that, Midas asked for permission to use the wood, and after two days of burning wood, they arrived in Queenstown at one o'clock in the morning. Midas boarded a train to Dublin, then caught a steamer to Liverpool. He was only six hours distant from London, and the time was twenty to twelve on the twenty-first. He was about to board a coach to London when suddenly a policeman appeared and said, "I arrest you in Queen Victoria's name!"

Midas was shocked he was in gaol nine hours before his deadline, the jewels he had were taken away, and Midas had a phone call to Jules and Jules replied, "Don't give up. You still have time."

He saw that he was wrong about the time when the clock outside struck one, and then an hour and a half later, the police arrived and said, "these jewels, where did you get them?"

"From Iceland, I found when I explored for Jules Verne?"

"And the pearls?"

"Off the coast of India."

"In that case, you are free to go. They have been catalogued, and if they are sold elsewhere, you will be arrested."

"Understood."

He arrived in London when Big Ben showed ten minutes before nine; he had lost by being late. Midas went to an inn and slept that night and morning. He woke up around seven-thirty and looked at his watch, it showed London time and then got a paper that was at the door and read the headlines and saw that it was Saturday the twenty-first, he had gained a day, he dashed outside caught a train and arrived at Jules at quarter to nine, Jules Verne beamed and said "well done, but you were in Liverpool yesterday what took you so long?"

"I didn't realise I went across the dateline until too late; I only remembered when I saw the newspaper."

They laughed as they ate in celebration.

Midas's trip didn't end there for the next few years, Midas continued to inspire Jules Verne with tales of the unknown, but Midas gained to like Jules that he was still acting young, especially after his adventure to unknown coordinates to see what the weather was like, Midas had come back from the coordinates of thirty-four degrees fifty-seven-minute South and one hundred fifty degrees and thirty minutes West to say the hurricanes were deadly. After a few years, and Midas was meant to be fifty-seven, and Jules was showing more than him, he left in the year eighteen eighty-five.

US Making History

Midas left for America using the balloon used to cross Africa, with only his satchel of books, jewels, pearls, staff, Indian outfit, undershirt, and watch. He sailed above the land of the United Kingdom. However, the winds and storms blew him day and night in darkness. For forty days, it rained and lightning, causing Midas to be wearing nothing but scorched clothes by the time he landed on the waters of the Pacific Ocean, overshooting his target by over five thousand kilometres. He was rescued by a ship that, unknowingly, were pirates. But once he awoke to find himself tied up and his satchel was empty, he knew he was rescued by the wrong hands; he used a sharp instrument to escape the ropes and find his staff. He climbed above the deck and saw his jewels being examined. He went over, knocked the pirate out and grabbed his belongings. He found a boat and jumped in; lowering the boat to the water, he rowed away from the ship. Bullets were fired until the captain shouted, "Forget him; he is going to die once he arrives in Hawaii." The last words were drowned out by the waves, and soon Midas was knocked overboard and blacked out. The pirates left him for Midas was dead and buried on the island of Hawaii as far as they were concerned. Mitchell laid there unconscious for many days, stranded. Beside him was his leather satchel containing; his undershirt, his staff, some precious stones and a dozen books in purses. When Mitchell woke up, he moved from the coast and staggered to the trees for shelter. A few minutes later, he suddenly heard a chorus of angry people speaking in a language he guessed was their local language. "Malihini, Kanaka 'e, haole," the loudest of them all was a female voice which said "Haole, 'ilipuakea!"

"Sorry, I don't understand; how long have I been on this island?"

A voice spoke in perfect English, "Six months, maybe more"

Midas looked up and said, "What year is it?"

"It is the year eighteen eighty-six."

"Where am I?"

"Hawaii on the island of Kaua'i"

"May I stay for a while? Got nowhere else to go!"

"Sure, you are free to stay."

Midas stayed on the islands of Hawaii for another fourteen years under the new name of Makaio. He cleaned up and learnt their way of life, and when it was the beginning of the year nineteen hundred and Mitchell was fourteen hundred years old almost; he travelled to the west coast of America.

On arriving, the Americans asked for identification, and Midas knew he was a dead man, so he said, "Was robbed at sea by pirates, escaped with my items of value; however I have lost all signs of my identity, all I know is that I am thirty-three years old, my birthday is in February and was called Mark Gladd."

"Well, come and get you some papers to sign to be a citizen. Do you have any relatives?"

"I have a younger brother, but I haven't heard from him in years."

After Mark Gladd got registered, he found a place to rest and went to a room. On his way to his room, a man came over and asked, "Sorry to be rude, but you remind me of a person that caught a train from East to West of America. I was young at the time, but your face is in my head" Mark turned to see a man in his fifties staring at him.

"Many people have the same face almost, you could be mistaken, but I am not offended."

For the next few years under the reign of Theodore Roosevelt, Mark travelled with his new passport and a new job as a portrait painter. Mark lived in the Bay of San Francisco, and on the seventeenth of December, nineteen hundred three - two years into his new job - he arrived in North Carolina at a place called Kitty Hawk. He spotted a man in a flying machine. Mark whistled and spoke to no one in particular, "What do you know, Leonardo was right, man can fly, and so was Jules Verne." The plane was twenty feet above the wind-swept beach. Mark watched as the flight lasted twelve seconds and covered one hundred twenty feet. Mark rushed over and met the two men responsible for this sight. The two men spotted him. After introductions, Mark discovered that Orville Wright was the one to have piloted the first powered airplane. Mark watched as they took turns, for three more flights were made that day with Orville's brother Wilbur piloting the record flight lasting fifty-nine seconds over a distance of eight hundred fifty-two feet. Mark painted a couple of pictures and then went back home. After another few years, Mark was now pretending to be thirty-nine, after making his birthday February fifteenth, when at five twelve in the morning on Wednesday the eighteenth of April, a massive earthquake shook the state of California. Mark woke up to the sounds of screaming and the smell of smoke. Looking out of his window, he spotted what appeared to be a cloud of smoke and dust. Mark rushed out to see that the whole city of San Francisco, under the blanket of smoke and whole buildings, was falling like sticks, Mark tried to help people, and after three days, he was one of the survivors of a most devastating event, with his things intact. Mark moved to Michigan and worked with a man named Henry Ford, who had been trying to make a car affordable and efficient for the past three years. Mark helped out with his knowledge dating back to Leonardo, and in the year nineteen hundred eight, Model T was advertised with drawings done by Mark and was sold. Cars became a thing for everyone, not for the wealthy. William Taft became President the very next year. Mark having trouble hiding his age, moved north to Canada and back again, pretending to be his long-lost brother Matthew Gladd and Mark decided to spend time with his new nephew. Matthew arrived during Wilson's reign as president, and soon Matthew was signed up for war after the assassination in Austria; three years into it, Matthew was rushed over to France to help out.

Matthew arrived in France and was told to help the Allies fight the Germans. He shot and dodged the bullets and, after months, decided to run out and bring back some of the injured soldiers. He pulled out his staff and shouted, "For the Allies and for America" he charged out and, with his staff, deflected the bullets. Some grazed him, but he was healed and carried on. A storm gathered, and Matthew decided to use the storm to his advantage. He raised his staff and, like a javelin, tossed the staff into the air. The lightning struck the staff and caused a flash of bright light; using the light as a distraction, he pulled the soldiers out of the warzone and safe in the ditches. Matthew ran out to collect more soldiers and retrieve his staff. He came back uninjured and shirtless. The soldiers were shocked and wondered what happened on the battlefield. It was nearing the end of the year, and Matthew saw more and more people killed while he wasn't. He stopped doing it until one morning in summer when more and more troops arrived from America, and more and more were wounded that Matthew ran out again. He charged to collect fellow Americans; the dust filled the battlefield, and Matthew felt the bullets rip through his flesh and the blood flow stop as it healed, he pulled men from the ground and supported them, and as he arrived back at the trenches, the allies saw as the dust cleared a scene like no other. Matthew was shirtless and unscathed, and the men he brought back were safe. When the war ended that year, Matthew returned home with the twelve million, eight hundred thirty-one thousand, five hundred wounded who were mourning over the five million, five hundred twenty-five thousand that died. He made a new home in New Jersey when he arrived back in America, shocked by the anger of the men he had seen. He prayed to the Lord that he would be around for any more tragedies like this.

When Matthew pretended to be fifty, he decided to move north by boat to Canada and returned a few years later, aged thirty. He arrived in New York in the year nineteen thirty-six. Mitchell moved around New York City, visited the Statue of Liberty and painted pictures from the top of the Empire State building. Mitchell was overwhelmed by the recovery rate the world was doing after the war that happened a few decades back. One night, Mitchell closed his eyes and went back to all the events that happened while being in America that weren't devastating. *Mitchell remembered going into the cinemas when he first saw what they were and remembered watching the turnouts; he remembered going to the library and then to the book store after reading the books by Brothers Grimm and taking a few for further reading. Mitchell remembered riding the car and watching the world around him change. His memory went back to the earthquake and seeing the woman standing in the distance as he ran from the city. He remembered seeing her again during the war.* He woke up after hearing over the radio that a large blimp burned up in the sky above the state of New Jersey. He decided to revisit California and arrived in Hollywood the following month. It was June when he went around and soon spotted a name that made him smile. It was Walt Disney, the founder of Mickey Mouse, a show that made Mitchell feel young again, considering his age. Donald Duck and Pluto along with Goofy, made Mitchell feel what it was like to be a child, and he went to find the famous man, but when he heard about a full-length feature film coming out in six months, he decided to wait for Walt to come. While staying in a hotel, Mitchell learned that a girl born and raised in Kansas who had moved around most of her life learnt to fly and decided to take a trip around the world. He followed her progress with some others as she and a man named Fred Noonan left Miami on June first. He listened as they stopped in South America, Africa, India, and Southeast Asia; they arrived at Lae, New Guinea, on June twenty-ninth. Mitchell, who travelled the world twice, calculated that she had travelled about twenty-two thousand miles if the journey had been completed. When July came, he heard that Amelia Earhart had lost radio contact and disappeared near Howland Island.

Mitchell went to the Carthay Circle Theater in December for the premiere; he was blown away by the cleverness of Walt and immediately set out to find him since he didn't show. He went to the Biltmore Bowl in March the following year in nineteen thirty-eight, when he heard that Walt Disney was attending, to see Disney win an award for Old Mills. Mitchell bumped into Disney during the event and had a conversation with him. The two became close mates, and when Disney moved to Burbank to open his studio, Mitchell was hired to help paint the building and became a draft drawer for him. He was a part of Walt Disney's Studios, and Walt spoke one morning to his members and asked on the progress of their next two ones he was producing. Mitchell politely asked for the script of his next film, and Walt handed him the words to Pinocchio, and he said: "This is based on Carlo Collodi's story of Pinocchio. It should be nearly finished, I imagine so is Dumbo, which is about an elephant."

"I read Pinocchio, I think, at the library; I see that as a story of man and God. What about you?"

"I, too see it has a moral and a perspective of faith, but I am creating based on the story, so I don't know how Carlo wrote it."

When it came out the next year in February the seventh, Mitchell watched the premiere of Pinocchio and soon after that went to continue work on the Bambi. When Germany invaded Holland and France and people were worried about another war, Dumbo came out in October and Mitchell was one of many that turned up however when December came. Japan had attacked Hawaii with a bombing at Pearl Harbor causing America to declare war on Japan, which meant Disney was instructed to create instructional films. After sticking around for the premiere of Bambi, Mitchell was recruited and was sent to North Africa, where he refused to fight the natives. Mitchell spoke in their native language, warning the locals to hide and find safety. He used his staff to defend the natives, and when the Egyptians saw him attacking with a stick, they called him "Moses", for he walked into the Red sea and used lightning to attack many of the invading armies from both Italy and Iraq. Mitchell retreated to Casablanca, where Franklin Roosevelt and Churchill arrived to speak. After that, Mitchell flew from Casablanca to New York, where he heard over the radio that Saludos Amigos was released with poor results. Mitchell was then shipped to Italy in July after he found more men. He prayed to the Lord as he headed towards Sicily that his descendants were not getting involved, unaware that some were in the war. He arrived in July on the fourteenth and, with his staff and sword, shouted in perfect Italy, to the Americans' surprise,

"Soldati attenzione, ho il sangue dei gladiatori e la mente degli Dei" which meant "Soldiers beware, I have the blood of Gladiators and the mind of Gods"

One American shouted to him as they stormed Sicily, "What did you say to them? Some are scared?"

"I told them about my ancestors." With that, he fought. It wasn't until late August that Mitchell stormed the Italian area to rescue the wounded, he came back shirt riddled with bullet holes and covered with blood, but there was no sign of a wound on him. The soldiers he carried were alive as he placed them down and turned back to rescue more, mines exploded around him, but Mitchell continued to save the injured, he carried them back, and the survivors called out in awe, "He's immortal, he carries on with no sign of injury." Mitchell was with the injured as they returned to America via Spain.

After a year of resting, Mitchell pretended to be in the forties when he was sent to Japan to help free the captives there. He was only there for a few weeks when word was that Roosevelt had died, and soon after, Germany surrendered, leaving Japan in the fight. Mitchell rescued hundreds of people. Still, after a few months, an atomic bomb dropped on Hiroshima, killing eighty thousand people. Mitchell remembered the man behind the science of the atomic bomb and thought what Albert Einstein had to be thinking as he was a citizen of the opposing country. It was the sixth when the bomb hit, and Mitchell saw the mushroom from where he was; after three days, he saw another mushroom in the place known as Nagasaki. Days later, after the Soviet Union declared war, Japan surrendered.

Mitchell returned to America and moved to Los Angeles after seeing how Disney was going and was told he was in the progress of making a few more, including; Song of the South, Make Mine Music, Fun & Fancy Free. Mitchell resigned from the Company and began a free life in retirement and in hiding. He only came out to see the premieres, and when King George the sixth passed away, Elizabeth became Queen. Mitchell came out from hiding as Morris; he found a job as a painter and painted signs and walls to remodel the place after the war. After five months, he was told that a jet plane had left London. Morris then continued to work, and after another year, it was June, and everyone was gathering around the radio or television for the coronation of the Queen. Morris was lucky to have a television, and he watched the Queen leave and head into the crowd and towards the Abby. Morris thought he caught a glimpse of a woman who looked like his angel, but she didn't appear again on screen after the camera rolled away. Morris was impressed with the new Queen and then remembered his meeting with the other Queen. Days went by, and the word was spread of two brave men, Edmund Hillary and Tenzing Norgay, that scaled Mount Everest. And even after that, Morris heard something which made him believe there was an antidote to his curse. When given a chance to go to France, Morris decided to travel to help out. He took it because he realised he was around to help. For the next few years, Morris observed what was happening; television changed to colour, and progress was made on cars and planes. He went to see Elvis Presley and the new style of music, rock and roll. He bought a few books written in the United Kingdom called "The Lion, the Witch and the Wardrobe, Prince Caspian, The Voyage of the Dawn Trader, The Silver Chair, The Horse and His Boy, The Magician's Nephew and The Last Battle; however, he read them in a different order, this was in the year fifty-six.

A few years later, Queen Elizabeth toured Canada and the United States, and Morris was lucky enough to see her. Alaska and Hawaii become states of America, giving it a grand total of fifty-two. Suddenly it was nineteen sixty, and Kennedy was President of America and word was after a few Prime Ministers in Australia. The policy of Aboriginal and Englishmen was still held, and the population had a mixture of Indigenous in their blood. The Prime Minister's team consisted of pure, half-and-half Aboriginals and pure Australians. News from Germany that the Berlin Wall was built between East and West, and a Russian named Yuri Gagarin became the first man in space. Morris had seen most movies, including Disney's productions of "The Adventures of Ichabod and Mr Toad", "Cinderella," "Treasure Island" "Alice in Wonderland," "The Story of Robin Hood and His Merrie

Men," "Peter Pan," "The Sword and the Rose", "Rob Roy: The Highland Rogue" and when Morris watched the Disney version of "20,000 Leagues Under the Sea" he laughed at how it made the book look unreal, he watched "Lady and the Tramp," "Davy Crockett, King of the Wild Frontier," "Littlest Outlaw," "The Great Locomotive Chase," "Davy Crockett and the River Pirates," "Westward Ho, The Wagons!" as well as "Old Yeller," "Sleeping Beauty," "Shaggy Dog" "101 Dalmatians" and even "Parent Trap." Morris watched most of the movies that came out and even painted a few of their posters. Morris was soon getting 'older" and decided to stay in his room for most days. He listened to the radio as the world moved on.

Morris listened as the world around him changed, but after the death of Monroe in sixty-two, Morris found something new and interesting to read. It was the year nineteen sixty-three, and a comic had been realised by Marvel, originally called Timely Publications. It was about a boy bitten by a radioactive spider; Morris read the comic after buying one of the first ones to come out and went to buy the first comic of other volumes called Fantastic Four and Hulk. Morris had collected Detective Comics, including Superman, Batman, Flash, Green Lantern, and others. After earning and spending money as a Private Investigator, Morris

walked into the comic shop one September to buy the
Avengers comics when a girl was first in line with a lot of
money, trying to buy a bunch of comics. "I demand you hand
me over one of each comic that has been released in the past
year!"

"Not until you vouch for how you have that much money in
your bag, for a girl your age can't be that rich."

"I tell you, sir; I earned this money the hard way."

"How?" asked the man

Morris coughed and said, "I will vouch for her; she helped me
on a case. I assume some of the money she earned. I say she
has enough, for each comic is fifteen cents, and I counted
over two hundred in the past year, including Fantastic Four,
Hulk and even some DC one."

The girl was surprised when she looked at her money. Morris
counted fifty dollars, more than enough, "Sorry for the mix-
up," the girl smiled, and the man gave her a box of comics,
she walked out, and Morris bought his comic and soon
followed. At the time, Morris was wearing a fedora and a
long jacket. He smiled and said, "Name's Morris Gladd,
Private Eye of Los Angeles. How did you get that money?"

"As I told the man, I earned it; thanks for vouching for me,
but I better get home before my parents freak out." the girl
replied before heading into the busy streets. The following

month, while Morris talked to the owner as he was buying comics, the girl returned and waited in the queue.

"Have you heard, I can't wait for it to come to America, but the Brit I spoke to says it's fabulous," Morris began. "They started a series called Doctor Who about a time traveller doing missions for his people."

He left and finally noticed the same girl in the shop, and for the next ten years, Morris, before he changed identity, saw the same girl in the same shop.

It was nineteen sixty-nine, and Morris was at home getting ready to think of a way to change from Morris to his son when he went out and bought a new television and watched during that year as the first man landed on the moon. After that, it was the seventies, and Morris was no longer himself. He fled in seventy-two and returned as Marvolo. Marvolo continued in his father's work, and it was the year that Ireland lost many people during Bloody Sunday.

Marvolo travelled the globe. He lived during the seventies and the eighties, and Marvolo was there at the beginning of the nineties. He went around the world, watching, reading and observing as the world changed. He was there when the Berlin War collapsed; he watched the beginning and the end of Doctor Who, and he watched his collection of Disney movies on VHS when they were remastered. It was the year nineteen ninety-five, and Marvolo went through all he had seen and read.

Marvolo had been buying VHSes of all Disney that had been released since the year nineteen eighty-five, which were after watching some of them at the theatre. He ran into a twenty-one-year-old woman about a hundred times as he entered a theatre around America. He watched more movies than he could have counted and read more books than he ever thought possible. When it was the year nineteen ninety-five, he spent over a grand on videos and movies, watched over a hundred movies, and read over a thousand books. Marvolo remembered entering London in the year nineteen ninety-three and walking around and running into a lady named Rowling who was writing down parts for a book series, Joanne, who was twenty-eight and Marvolo, who was acting fifty. After ten minutes and a coffee, she explained her theories and then asked for an unusual name, and Marvolo said: "Why not use my name?"

Joanne agreed, and after a few years of talking via letters, Marvolo was told that a book was coming out soon. He received the letter in early nineteen ninety-six, and Marvolo was getting tired of pretending to be old and was ready to leave. He decided to head towards London to visit J.K. Rowling one last time since he was earning money for being a

Private Investigator and caught a plane over to Paris first. He planned then to fly over to London. He had a house full of supplies and a suitcase full of history. As he flew, he looked at his staff, remembered all he had lived through, and then saw that he still had the same undershirt with a pattern that was a map. He hasn't buried anything since he bought a house and became PI, and then as he landed in Paris, he decided to spend a year there. It was August thirty-first in the year ninety-seven when he heard a crash. He ran over and saw a car crash and heard people saying, "That was Princess Diana!" as the ambulance took away an injured lady, Marvolo remembered hearing about the divorce and reading the papers. He went over to get a closer look when someone spotted him and said, "You're Marvolo Gladd, aren't you the private investigator? What are you doing in Paris?" Marvolo spotted a girl aged twenty-four look up and walk away. "Sightseeing", and minutes later, he was chasing down the car owner. Marvolo found out that it was shipped from Germany.

He travelled Europe, and then by the time he got to London, it was the year nineteen ninety-nine. J.K. Rowling had already released three books. On July tenth, he entered the book store, and Joanne was there with a signing. She looked up and said: "Marvolo, you looked worn out; you sent word you were coming, but it has been two years. What took you so long?"

"I was investigating the 'accident' of Princess Diana in Paris", she sighed and said, "I have the books for you signed and waiting. I kept them since I knew you would show up." He left the shop after a hug and a talk. Marvolo was around when the Euro was launched throughout Europe, and he caught a plane back to America. He went back home and changed his name to act as Marvolo's son Mason. Mason read the first two books that year, and when he got to the part in which Tom was named after his grandfather, making him Tom Marvolo Riddle, Mason laughed at what she wrote in the book at the front "Hoping you have a magical life full of adventure and love, J.K." Mason cried. He then read the third book. It was the end of nineteen ninety-nine, and the people were complaining about the date being double zero. As the clock ticked towards midnight, Mason prayed, "Lord, I have lived fourteen hundred and ninety-nine years and have seen the rise and fall of great people, made friends with all sorts of people and even made friends with an author of great literacy, I will pray that I continue to live until I find a real purpose for being on this earth instead of just being an inspiration to people that became famous." The clock chimed

Midnight and Mason smiled. "The world is still spinning!" he praised the Lord and closed his eyes.

Age of Technology

Mason changed professions, decided to be a fireman, trained up, and was given the job after three months. Since the seventies, with the banning of Chlorofluorocarbons and hydrofluorocarbons, fridges still were found and destroyed. It was July eighth, and Harry Potter was released in stores when Mason was on duty during the day with a fire in Manhattan, so he couldn't get a book. However, when he returned home after the long hour of fighting the fire, was a parcel on the doorstep; inside the parcel was the fourth book and on the inside cover was her writing saying, "To the son of Marvolo, Mason. Enjoy reading, Rowling." Mason smiled and read the letter that went with it and cried, thinking about all the lies he told, but no one cared, as long as it was a person that cared for them. He went to bed and had a strange dream of the twenty-four-year-old woman who was at the crime scene of Diana's death. He woke up and continued his rounds, rescuing cats from trees. Mason Granger (asked for his last name to be changed after reading Harry Potter four) played chess in the station when the sirens went off. There was a house fire in the Bronx; he stopped playing and dashed out. The four-storey house was burning brightly when they arrived. Mason heard screams from inside and knew someone was in there. He dashed in and saved the people inside the burning building without his suit. When he came out, his clothes were scorned, and the people were covered with ash, but Mason had no injuries. He was given a medal of bravery, and he was given enough money to update his house.

For the next year, Mason recorded and watched dozens of shows; from the beginning of June, he watched *Even Stevens, SpongeBob SquarePants, CatDog, Doug, Rugrats,* and *Wild Thornberrys.* Mason was happy with no company, home alone and watching shows repeated and new ones on the American Broadcasting Channel and CBS and NBC to pass the time. It was soon another year, and posters for movies were coming out, including Harry Potter and the 'Sorcerer's Stone', and he decided to save time to watch that. After spending time at home in front of the television, watching shows such as Sabrina, Charmed and Crime Scene Investigation or going to the library to borrow new books. He went over to Australia to check what was going over there during the winter. When he arrived to see that outside the Parliament House was the statue of Max still standing. He went to Sydney and overheard that the United Party had won the election after the Olympics (which Mason couldn't go to, the first time in 32 years). The Leader Woorin

(Warrin) Simons, whose father's side was pure aboriginal, and his mother's side was a mixture, made it that any person from overseas was welcome as long as they obeyed the rules written by Max and the previous governments. Mason saw that every house was about thirteen feet above the ground, except for stadiums and pools. He saw that Caucasian, Indigenous, Greek or Chinese people were in harmony. He smiled, thinking that he had made a difference. He saw that the roads were dirt tracks, and cars easily drove between trees. He caught a taxi to a hotel and ran into a person. He looked at her and said, "Hello, I'm Mason."

The girl looked up and said, "Sorry, my name is Suki. I am sorry...."

"I was the one that bumped you. I am sorry, I shall say something though. Can you please point me in the direction of the city's best sites, for I am from America, here for the winter?"

"Well, I shall say, check the Bridge, Opera House and the bay. That land was only permitted to change and be built on the ground?"

"How long have the buildings been above ten feet up?"

"As long as I could remember, I came after World War Two, well my family did, my grandmother was forty at the time, and my mother was only twelve."

"Thanks, I shall see this bridge!" Mason left and saw the sites and then found a place to post a letter to his station. Mason then took the plane to Melbourne. After seeing the sites, including the Twelve Apostles, he overheard that the first train successfully travelled from Dromana to Smithton, which was in Tasmania, only last month. Mason arrived in Dromana and bought himself a ticket to Smithton on the Comeng Bilby. After going down underground at a slow descent of one in thirty, he finally was underwater. He saw the lights and the super-strong glass which was holding back the water. He arrived in Smithton after four hours. He walked around and saw the chocolate factory and then caught a plane after seeing his statue again and arrived in Perth. He then spent days there and arrived back in America on September first. It was his month off, and after catching up on television and news, he was walking around New York one morning for breakfast when a plane was heading straight for the World Trade Center. Mason was already at the base when the building started to collapse and go up in smoke when two planes crashed. The fire brigade and ambulance were there as soon as possible, but Mason was already in the building and running up. He climbed the stairs and tried to find people when suddenly he heard a boy cry out "Mother!" he saw a boy trapped under a slap of concrete and saw him pointing to a door blocked off by metal. He turned to the boy and said, "Is your mother in there?"

"She went in to get some papers, sir; I can't feel my leg."

Mason lifted the slab and said, "Get to the window and wait there." Mason saw the beams and, using maths and physics, managed to move the beams away to open the door. He pulled the lady out and took her to the window, the ceiling was collapsing, and the boy was using Mason's staff to help himself stand up. Mason looked around and saw what appeared to be a large curtain and had an idea. He channelled the creativity of MacGyver and then tied a chair to the curtain and shouted, "Get on. Is there anyone else on this floor,"

"Dunno' the boy groaned. Mason helped the boy on the chair and told the mother to stand behind it and take the two ropes; the chair had wheels. Mason said, "I will search for other survivors, tell the police that Mason saved you and is still looking" he pushed the chair out the window, and the curtain created a glider like he had seen on Australian beaches and watched as the chair gliding towards the ground. He ran back in and searched, he found a few injured people and grabbed them and carried them towards a window, he was only fifty floors up, and he couldn't go on any more, he sighed as he ran out the window with only his staff attached to his belt and four people holding on, he jumped and as he plummeted towards the ground, opened his backpack up and watched as the people on the ground stared in awe as the large plastic sheet opened to create a parachute. He landed ten miles from the crash site, and the doctors and police rushed over to help, Mason explained and then went onwards to help the firemen. After that day, Mason was in mourning, he stayed home for a month, and after watching Harry Potter, he moved to Los Angeles and became a part of their fire department.

Staying in the city of Angels, Mason was pretending to be in the forties when he attended the Primetime Emmy Awards in Shubert Theatre on November fourth after a Halloween night. He walked around and ran into an Australian actor, Hugh. Mason recognised him from X-Men and, after a quick greeting, asked, "What is it like to play this hero, the man that can't get injured."

"I really like playing the character. I feel like I can be him?"

After the Academy Awards at the Kodak Theatre on March twenty-fourth, Mason found himself walking around only to be spotted by Brian Singer. After ten minutes, Mason was called to be an extra in a film that was being made. When Mason saw Hugh again, he realised this was the sequel to X-Men and was really excited. After being a couple of people in the background, Mason left for his hotel when he got a phone call from the fire department "Fire in a cinema, how close are you to..." Mason got the address and found a motorcycle and drove off.

Mason was busy with prank fires and real threats for the next few years. He went to the cinemas to see the Marvel movies and a few others, including Disney's Treasure Planet, Cinderella, Santa Clause and Peter Pan two. He saw himself in Pirates of the Caribbean with Johnny Depp. After the Olympics in Athens, the year was soon two thousand and six. Mason watched Johnny Depp in his sequel of 'Pirates of the Caribbean' and Hugh's third role as Wolverine in 'X-Men: The Last Stand'. He watched Daniel Craig perform the role of James Bond, and after he watched David Tennant play his second year of The Doctor in the Runaway Bride, the New Year began.

For the next six years, Mason watched the actors he made friends with turn stars and watched as Marvel and Disney, and DC created film after film. He visited Britain and Australia after Perth and Adelaide were connected with an underwater railway. He shook hands with stars from Down Under and the United Kingdom. Mason was nearly pretending to be fifty when he came home to watch Thor Two at the cinema. Being on call around America, Mason was known as the Fire Ranger. He watched The Wolverine with Hugh Jackman thirteenth year in the same role, Avengers Two, and a few Disney movies. He was impressed with the broadcasting shows; Castle, Bones, Mentalist, and even NCIS were all still rolling, and the new shows of late, such as Once Upon a Time, were getting numbers of viewers. As this was happening, Mason noticed the more creative the books and movies were and how technology was playing a huge part, including the newest technology way to become fit, the DIGAME. He retired and travelled around the world and, after seven years, arrived in the United Kingdom to see George Alexander Louis go to school for the first time. He went to his home for the year and after realising that he had; seven DVDs and two videos of Harry Potter, every DVD box set of Doctor Who including the eighth and ninth season, all James Bond on tape and DVD, all Chronicles of Narnia, the Percy Jackson set with four so far and even all Marvel and DVD in storage, that he better find a new hobby. It was twenty-twenty, and with the Olympics coming up in Perth, he decided to watch the games. On the trip over, he thought back at what he did as he travelled the globe and how no one recognised him too much. Mason decided to leave that life and try out for boxing for the next Olympics.

With a new identity Mac Gyser, he joined boxing, and after four years, he flew with the people to Thailand for the Olympics. He won two gold medals. When he heard about the UN having an emergency meeting, he went over and spied on the meeting. The UN had the presidents, prime ministers and the leaders of the world there, and someone spoke up, "We are destroying the planet with our carbon emissions. We need to think of methods to reduce this?"

"We are trying to plant more trees."

Suddenly a voice spoke from the masses, "Rooftop gardens" the crowd parted, and George was standing there with a drawing of a childlike building with trees and flowers and said, "Have gardens for the birds to rest on their flights."

There was silence, and suddenly Solomon, the Prime Minister of Australia from the United Party, clapped and said: "We have already taken that to some extent ever since Max told us to build our houses above or in line with the trees."

President Obama said, "America has the most buildings that reach the sky. Planting trees up there sounds marvellous, but what about the cost."

"It doesn't cost much to plant trees, just time," The Queen said. "I am ninety-eight years old, but I can still plant trees in our garden."

"Aren't you retired?"

"Not until I reach one hundred in two years," Elizabeth said proudly

Mac saw someone step out, he was around twenty-five years old, step forward and say, "As the representative of Dr Forrest from the Tree and Plant Rejuvenation Process in America, I am happy to say there are enough seeds to regrow an entire forest if we have to, in the warehouse."

"Where is Dr Forrest, may I ask?" Prince Charles asked, standing old but fit, "and the question is will we be around to see their work?"

"It will take ten years to grow, but they will be there for the next centuries, with the right care."

"Are they going to cause lightning?" asked William and Henry in unison.

"They wouldn't cause the building to burst into flames if that is what you are asking."

Twenty minutes later, they agreed that with the delivery of local and native trees, rooftop gardens would be constructed for the next few decades. After that, Solomon said that the work into new rail roads, using magnetism, was in process. That population has reached a new high with the inland being turned into sky risers with the ground still untouched. This was in all parts except the radius around Uluru. After that meeting, Charles spotted Mac and said, "Aren't you the famous boxer? How come you are here,"

"Lost!"

"Well, I got a job for you. My grandson will be entering high school in two years, and the queen will be retired, giving me the throne. I will need someone to watch over him for the next six years. Can you be that person?"

"As in, come back in two years and then teach at the school and be a secret bodyguard?"

"You will have to be there before he starts to build up a reputation, but yes, can you do that, Mac?"

Mac flew to London and taught at the high school where George was enrolled. For the next eight years, Mac taught PE, and when George came and watched over him, no one tried to kill him, but he was there when he was picked on for being a royal. It wasn't until George finished high school that he retired and was assigned to be his guard until George was twenty-one. Mac left and sailed to find a new home and new life in the year twenty thirty-four.

Mitchell found that he was nearly fifteen hundred thirty-four this coming New Year, and he was running out of cover stories. He was sick of lying and fleeing. He bought a ship and a submarine and christened the boat Lady Truth and the submarine Lady Adelaide. Then he decided to dig up his past and set sail and only touch land on the south pole.

As he sailed, unknown to him, the world began to change. When King Charles retired in the year twenty forty-eight, King William took over. Technology was advancing so much that William, aged, sixty-six, stopped all advances and asked that everything was to be caught up, meaning all videos and DVDs were converted to Blu-ray. All the music was converted to one type. This took as long as George and his firstborn James were on the throne. the technology was steady, coal was depleting, and by the end of the year twenty-one forty-five, the bachelor King made it that this was the way to save the world. His sister Victoria took the throne aged eighty-eight and continued the wish for twelve more years. The eldest son Stuart took over trying to finance the magnetic levitation tracks, which Australia managed to do during the stabilisation. It took Queen Bess or Elizabeth the third to have the whole world's train system off the ground literally after twenty per cent of the world died from an outbreak killing children under the age of five and adults over eighty. Doctors tried to find a cure for all diseases using zebrafish DNA using the remains of research found in Australia. During this time, Mitchell sailed and submerged, only to stop on the ice of Antarctica after following the map on his shirt to find his past in Iceland and in Hastings. He re-read his book and then wrote the sequel. He looked at the chess pieces and cried over the play. It was the year twenty-two hundred when Bess retired, giving the throne to thirty-five-year-old the youngest daughter after the other three triplets died before retirement. MG decided to head towards Australia and after two hundred sixteen years of sailing, arrived in Sydney to find the year twenty-two hundred and fifty and stepping into the harbour saw, the buildings topped with trees and cars driving along dirt tracks but trains floating a foot above the ground, he entered the city. He saw people staring at the televisions. Mitchell found a hotel, booked a room, and noticed that everyone was busy. He saw the calendar to see it was the sixteenth of June. He decided to see what he had missed by reading a newspaper to find that all papers had converted to tablets. He grabbed what was called a tablet lite, which was free to guests, and read that the New Queen Diana, which was the great, great-granddaughter of King George the seventh, had turned the Castle into an orphanage and foster home for she could not have children, then when he turned on the flat screen which was what everyone had, all old stuff was converted and recycled, to find that a World Lottery was being drawn by a computer. With the prize over a million dollars, it was the four hundred sixty-eighth time making it nineteen years of being drawn. The prize was over a billion, the population was steady at eight billion, and the counter at the bottom showed the whole population were viewers. The population was lowered rapidly according to what was called the mist of death during the reign of Queen Bess, killing over one billion people worldwide, cutting both China and India in half. As the lottery was drawn and the machine announced no winner, Mitchell left the hotel and found a restaurant to buy dinner. He overheard that Real Life has just bought Nickelodeon and is trying to buy another. Mitchell went back to the hotel to find that half the channels were operational unless paid with a credit card. When Mitchell found the history channel saw everything he missed in five days of staring at the screen non-stop, eating food that he ordered and was delivered. He learned that there had been two outbreaks since he sailed; both started in China. One was radiation went airborne, which was the 'Mad hatter' epidemic killing eight per cent of the world's population during the King James (2120-2125), then again in the year twenty-one eighty to twenty-one ninety-nine with what was thought to be carbon monoxide from a chain reaction of volcanoes from St Helen' in the United States to Mount Etna in Italy and Mount Fuji in Japan causing a cloud to cover the world. Doctors tried using zebrafish DNA to save people from Parkinson's but failed when they died in surgery from CO poisoning. Scientists believed that the magnetic transportation caused the volcanoes to erupt. Mitchell remembered being in Antarctica during that time period. Years passed, and the lottery still hadn't been won, and Mitchell was free to be himself. Forty years later and, MagLev was being used on cars, and they began converting cars into solar-powered, reducing the use of carbon dioxide. King Andrew also stopped the production of paper and started using water to create electricity. Ten years later, cars were produced to be solar panelled roofs and were floating a foot above the ground. However, cars still need to be charged. Mitchell went into science during the time of King Andrew and worked with a scientist in France; after a decade of research and planning, Mitchell combined einsteinium-254 with zinc and created a stable element unless heated. They studied it and saw that it had a half-life of an hour. The energy was enough to run the building for a day. They tested it on a car and saw that this was enough for a month's car drive or more. Mitchell was happy, and when the rest of them asked for a name, he said, "Veranium after Jules Verne." They agreed, and with fifty years and the end of King David's reign, Veranium was used as a cell to power cars; the solar energy caused the cell to give the car power. During that time, the lottery was won by WWA. After one hundred years, over ninety billion American dollars were won and converted into credit and distributed. Hence, everyone had different amounts of credit but was considered rich, considering the world became in financial crisis after people were buying tickets twice a month. WWA converted his island into a printing press for notes and an automated bank for credit. By the time twenty-three eighty came, credit was used as a way to buy shows, and broadcasts for RLI stopped running certain channels.

Mitchell then decided to move to the North Pole and would come down once a year since cars, planes and even boats became energy efficient, with paper and coal becoming unusable. After seventy years of spending time at the North Pole, a doctor made a blind man see using DNA from an eagle, which spiked scientistic trying to use animal DNA to cure illness. Still, years of this caused people to die from unusual diseases such as bird disease. People were scared that in the years to come, RLI would ban cross-genetics; however, in the year twenty-five hundred, a boy was born that could control the wind, and this was only proven when he was ten.

Timeline of Tana

Over in Canada in the year twenty-four ninety-six, around midday on the twenty-ninth of February, a girl was heard crying. The child's mother looked up at her loving husband and smiled with tears in her eyes. "We have a daughter, Tana" The husband nodded. They left the hospital and caught an air-taxi from the hospital because of all the snow, Canada was as white as the Arctic, and the only way to travel was about ten feet in the air or higher. They headed home with Tana, who was three weeks at the time.

As they headed home over the snow, a wave of energy from the power plant rocked the cab, sent out an electromagnetic pulse, and turned off the engine. The cab was losing height, and as it fell, it began to tip, and the doors opened just as another wave of energy hit. The Canadian Power Plant melted down and imploded, Tana fell, and the father watched as the baby headed towards the centre of the explosion. Radiation which was harmless to adults, came in waves as the baby fell. The parents jumped when the driver shouted "Out", and the cab landed a meter away from the magnetic rails and crashed into the snow. The parents landed on the rails and rushed to where they hoped to find their baby and found the baby alive and crying miles away from the remains of the power plant.

Two years passed, and the site was cleaned up, and no damage from the radiation was evident except for cars that could not start within ten miles from the site. The power was returned to the city. Tana was learning to walk, and her parents were having trouble finding her when she began to walk. She was stumbling around the kitchen and ended up in the dining room the next minute or in the bathroom one minute and the next minute, crawling on the washing machine. After a year of walking and soon, her first full sentence was "Mum-me wat iz tha time?"

Soon Tana was five years old and was heading into an early learning centre for Canadian children. There, she learned hygiene, manners, social skills and how to read and write her name. Being born in February, Tana had just turned five when learning started in March; since the year twenty-three thirty-two, both hemispheres started school in March and had a break in June, October, and three months after Christmas. When summer came, it was June sixth; Tana came home and shouted, "We are going to New York!" She couldn't wait to see the Statue of Liberty. For the next few months, Tana began to take an interest in the past and asked her parents questions about what happened before she was born. When school began when she was six years old and in the first week of Foundation Year was asked by her teacher, "How many birthdays have you had" Tana replied, "One." "How come you only had one birthday Tana?" the teacher asked politely while the rest of the class laughed.

"I was born on the twenty-ninth of February", she replied.

"That makes sense, you are six years old, but you only had one actual birthday since your birthday is only every four years."

School was going well for her until term nearly ended, and the bell was about to ring. A couple of students in year three saw Tana and sneered, "If it isn't little miss teacher's pet always telling the teacher when she is meant to move on, my sister told us that you stopped her from finishing painting because it was time to count to ten, well let's see if you know how to count to ten." They picked up some stones and began to toss them at her, counting "One, Two, Three" just as the bell began to chime.

Tana ran away, wishing that she was home, and after a few seconds, she heard the sound of her cuckoo clock go off three times. She looked at the clock. The LCD lights flashed "15:00 Fri 2/6", and suddenly her dad shouted, "When did you arrive? We were both in the garden out back; she didn't even hear you come in, and how come school ended early."

Tana looked at her watch and saw that her watch blinked at her "15:05": School ended ten seconds ago according to her watch, but according to the sun (which she can tell time from in a heartbeat) saw that it was only three o'clock.

"Something wrong, Tana. You haven't answered my question."

"We had an early mark, I took an express bus home, and I didn't want to disturb you", Tana replied, trying to figure out what happened. She looked at her clock, which was never wrong and came to two conclusions "This is all a dream, the boys are still throwing rocks at me," or "I went back in time" suddenly as the clock changed to one passed, she realised that she did time travel for the clocks were in sync but two different times, one five minutes into the future. She waited five minutes, and she was still confused. She paced around the room and wished that time was back to normal and opened her eyes to see both clocks, the one on her wrist and the one on her wall, had the same time. Suddenly dad shouted, "you been silent for five minutes. Everything all right?"

"Fine, dad, just getting over the long term I have had." Tana walked downstairs, realising she could jump through time. They stayed home during the summer break, and Tana spent the first two weeks jumping back and forth in time trying to understand, she kept her watch as the true time, and when she went back, she always arrived to make it look like she was in the same time. She practised by going back in time to the shops and bought sweets and then arrived home, and no time passed. Tana only spent a minimum of two minutes in the past and arrived back thirty seconds maximum from the time she left, which she made up in the past later on. She was learning and by the time school started up again, she had mastered going back and forward two minutes, travelling around the town.

When Tana was ten, she decided to see how far back she could go and started expanding by a minute each practice until she reached thirty minutes. When Christmas came around, the perfect time arrived; it was Christmas morning. She woke up at seven o'clock and heard the parents snoring, she realised that she hadn't had a present for them both and thought about jumping back to eleven o'clock to when the "All U CAN BUY" was opened with last-minute gift ideas, after grabbing her portable bank-pocket drive, and suddenly found herself, outside their clock showing 11pm, she looked at her watch and saw it was 7:01 and knew her parents would be up at 7:40, she had thirty-three minutes to find the perfect presents, she dashed inside and went looking, she found a dress for mum and a holobook for dad and went to the counter and said, "Can I have these gift-wrapped, and hurry, I am on a time limit." Her watch was saying 7:27, and she had 7 minutes before she had to jump back. The lady behind the counter said, "That is eleven fifty credits or eleven eighty in cash."

Tana placed the pocket drive into the machine, and after scanning her fingerprint and typing in her pin code, she grabbed the gifts and checked her watch. "It was 7:32" she walked towards the door and into the snow-covered parking lot. She turned the corner into an alley and saw two boys following her; she checked her watch. As the seconds got closer to 7:34, she thought about home and being there at seven thirty-four and thought about jumping forward a total of eight hours and a minute forward. The boys watched as she turned the corner and vanished, and Tana arrived at the tree at 7:35. She placed the presents down and went into the kitchen. The parents came down and saw two new gifts and said, "Tana did you get up at midnight and place gifts under the tree."

"Yeh, I guess," Tana replied.

It was soon her birthday, and Tana wanted to celebrate her eleventh birthday on an actual day and thought about going back to twenty-four ninety-two and what was happening in L.A. and took a step forward and ended up seeing her clock show that it was six in the morning but, she was around nine o'clock in Hollywood. Unfortunately, not much was going on, she walked around and found a café and asked for pancakes, and the owner said: "Where're your parents?"

"They are at home. It's my birthday today. They let me go and buy my own breakfast."

"In that case, why don't I give you a treat? It's called the princess pile; it's strawberries, cream, chocolate and honey pancakes."

"How much is it?"

"For you, on the house, but I will take a tip of five dollars if you want."

"Here, and thanks."

Tana ate the pancakes when they arrived and then saw that it had been nearly fifty minutes. She thanked the owner, and walked out the door and into an alley. She thought about being home at six fifty-one and saw herself in the kitchen. She grabbed a plate, had some toast, drank some milk and when the parents got up at half-past, said: "Had breakfast already; we were thinking of making you pancakes."

"Can I have them for lunch? I have already eaten" she smiled and thought about her trip back into the past.

In the next few years, Tana entered higher learning and learned about early century history, between seventeen hundred and twenty-two hundred. Tana was learning a lot and, one lunchtime, asked the teacher, "What was life like in the eighteen hundreds?" The teacher replied, "We are only told what the books say."

Tana soon thought about travelling back to take looks; however, she realised she was still young. It was her thirteenth birthday, and the first grade of higher learning was over. She had a month to second grade; she decided to jump back to the year seventeen hundred forty-five France and found out that it was the time (according to History) of King Louis the fifteenth and a few days after the ball of Reinette, Reinette was moving in with him very soon, according to the rumours, Tana made a mental note to see what the ball was like when she is old enough. She went back to her time and continued to learn until she was seventeen years old.

It was Tana's seventeenth birthday when Tana learnt the consequences of jumping back in time, she decided to try to be at two places at once during the holidays, and she was with her parents. They had moved to New York. They were at a campsite, and one night, Tana woke up, checked her watch and then jumped back to morning at America's Smithsonian. She was walking around knowing that she had five hours.

Before she had to get back to the camp, she checked the date
on the wall clock and saw it was midday the very same
morning, she walked around and saw all the early century
history artefacts, and suddenly the alarm bells went off. Tana
saw a man chase a boy with a heavy-looking bag, something
fell out, and Tana realised the boy was attempting to steal
the enormous collection of natural gems and minerals. Tana
watched as the boy disappeared into the outside world and
vanished. Tana looked at her watch and saw it had been an
hour, she had an idea, she ran into the street and chased the
boy, the security guards had called the police and everyone
was running around the greenery of Washington. Tana kept
track of time as she followed the boy and finally caught up
with him; she tackled him as the police drew near. Tana
realised she was tired and needed sleep; she moved the bag
away from the boy tossing it a few inches into a bush, and
then let the boy go; the police arrived to see Tana run into
the trees, and the boy flee empty-handed and the gems safe
in a bush. Tana jumped forward in time and went to sleep. In
the morning, the radio told of a boy running large after trying
to take the Smithsonian's collection of gems and minerals
and of a girl who was seen running from the crime scene.
Tana realised she interfered with time, for she could not ever

come forward without compromising her whereabouts during the camp.

Tana spent the rest of the summer reading up on history and noticed that a massive section was missing in the library; using the internet on her holo-top, she found that pages were removed about the so-called "Doctor Who files," "Marvel files," and "DC Files" as well as others, but they were all rated unsafe. She decided to jump back to the year 1963, for that was the only date that kept popping back up; it was nearly July, so she had to get back soon. She quickly stepped back in time after dressing and changing the money to be for the appropriate time; she entered the busy streets of Los Angeles and found the drug stall. She entered and asked the man for the year's supply of comics that had come out so far; when the man looked at her strangely, she showed the money and said, "I can pay," the man looked shocked and asked, "What is your purpose here."

Tana yelled, "I demand you hand me over one of each comic that has been realised in the past year!"

"Not until you vouch for how you have that much money in your bag, for a girl your age can't be that rich." the man replied

"I tell you, sir; I earned this money the hard way."

"How?" asked the man

Someone behind her coughed and said, "I will vouch for her; she helped me on a case, I assume, some of the money she earned, does she have enough, for each comic is fifteen cents, and I counted over two hundred in the past year, including Fantastic Four, Hulk and even some DC ones, I say she has enough."

Tana was shocked and looked at her money; she had fifty dollars, more than enough; she miscalculated. "Sorry for the mix-up," she smiled. The man gave her a box of comics, she walked out, and the man soon followed, he was wearing a hat that was not very fashionable and a long jacket, he smiled and said: "Name's Morris, Private Eye of Los Angeles, how did you get that money?"

"As I told the man, I earned it; thanks for vouching for me, but I better get home before my parents freak out."

Tana left and watched as the man headed to a car. She turned the corner, returned to her room the next second, and hid the comics away. She planned to return next holiday, which would be next month in the past and collect some more.

During the next year, Tana returned to the same shop the same year or the following year, depending on which month it was, and bought more comics. When she jumped back and entered the drug store in the city of angels, she was surprised to see the PI there buying comics and talking to the man behind the counter. "Have you heard, I can't wait for it to come to America, but the Brit I spoke to says it's fabulous."

The little girl listened as the Private Eye mentioned Doctor Who and then, as he left, bought the comics and returned to her time. For the year of travelling, she collected a decade or more worth of comics and realised she couldn't hide them for much longer. She was nearly eighteen, and her parents thought of travelling to Los Angeles. When her birthday arrived, and she was heading to either university or finding a job, Tana had plans. In March, she was heading to university after getting a high mark and applied for History and Journalism. She was in university the first week when her parents told her they were leaving and were at the airport and asked where she was, she looked at the clock and saw she had an hour before her first class and lied saying "Near the airport, see you in a minute." She left her room and stepped into the toilet only to arrive near the airport; she hugged her parents and said goodbye. She watched them enter the plane. She walked away and vanished, arriving back at the toilet, making it look like she was there for ten minutes. She walked out and had her first lesson. After two two-hour lectures, she headed back to her room to see a man in the room. He turned and said: "I was told this was your room; I am assuming you are Tana?"

"Yes, why what happened?"

"Your parents boarded a Solarplane from New York to Los Angeles, correct?"

"WHAT HAPPENED?" Tana demanded

"The plane wasn't powered enough as the pilots hoped; the plane made it only as far as Utah."

"When did this happen?"

"An hour ago, the plane just dropped from the sky as the clouds covered the sun and the energy ran out, they landed in the desert."

"Give me a minute or two; I need to be alone" she ran into the ensuite, thought back one hour, and stepped into the past. She walked out behind the rocks that border Utah's desert, which is forbidden to have houses and saw the plane fall towards the ground. She stepped again and was in the toilet of the plane and stepped out and saw her parents smiling as they flew over Kansas and the clouds began to block the sun. Tana re-entered her ensuite five minutes later and took a deep breath. "I believe you, but why are you here?"

"I am from the United States Plane Officers, USPO, and on behalf of the people of New York Air Services, we are sorry fo...."

"I want you to get out; my parents have just died because someone didn't give the plane enough time to recharge; I suggest you find that person responsible and charge them with manslaughter." Tana stormed out and ended up in World War Two and then World War One, and she then found herself back in the present, and time hadn't changed much. The man exited the room, saw her down the corridor, and shouted: "If we find anything that belongs to them, do you want them?"

"That and the will, right now I need to study!"

The will was read, and Tana was given a large amount of credit, and the house was hers as well as the land; the USPO did find a necklace of an hourglass that Tana gave her mother for her birthday when she was fourteen, and the watch she given her dad, it was the old fashion fob watch. Tana looked at them, placed them on her, and said, "Time to make them proud!" she studied. As she learnt about history, she went back in time to collect books; she used the web to find out when the dates of the buildings were burned and bought the majority before the fires since books were a thing of the past and everyone now either has a holo-book which is a holographic copy of the book or the audio version which is just like watching a movie. Still, the characters are animated and not living. For three years since the crash, Tana studied and collected until she was twenty-one and had collected enough books to fill her whole house, where she had the books all stored; she needed a place to display them. She rang around and found land available but none of the right size; she then called up a service she saw in an ad "Angelo's Architectural Design and Carpeting, Billy Angelo, how may I help you?"

"I am Tana; I am looking for an area to build a library on."

"How big is the building?" Billy asked

"Um, I want it the size of the old colosseum", Tana begins, "40 high, horseshoe shape, but plus parking, makes in one twenty by one hundred maybe, size will be close to the ratio of the colosseum."

"Well, there was a building in North Dakota that was demolished; no one owns the property, for the person is trying to sell it."

"How big is the land area?"

"About one-fifty by one-fifty and plenty of trees for protection, so is that ok?"

"Perfect, I will be over there in a week. Let me just find a way to ship by books across."

She arrived on March sixteenth, and the Irish were getting ready for Saint Pats. Tana arrived at the area of land which had the remains of what looked like a studio or stadium and saw a young man in his thirties standing there looking at the land. And when she entered, he smiled. "I got your plans; I would be happy to build your library. The team are happy to help."

"That is lovely; I will be trying to open the library by next year, and will that be possible?"

"This should be done in eight months."

"That's great; I will be collecting more artefacts for the library. I need newspapers for the archives if possible; I will try to be back when it's finished."

"Excuse me, I may sound rude, but why are you building this?"

"My parents died, I loved history, and I need a way to keep myself moving on?

"Sorry to hear that."

Tana lied and caught the car back to the hotel she was staying at and decided to step back into the past starting from the year twenty-two, twenty-two, when newspapers became a thing of the past and go backwards a minute in each year, collecting a paper from their times, from America. As she vanished to collect the papers, Billy was building the skeleton of the building. Tana started in December 2222 and went back a minute a day to the seventeen century. She calculated that as ninety-five thousand five hundred forty-four days, which meant that many minutes which meant sixty-six days to collect them all, with rests and sleep, she estimated seventy-five days. And with that, she was off and back, it was now May thirtieth, and she returned to see the framework complete. She went over to Billy and said: "Nice work, so far, so good, so it consists of four to six floors of varying heights. That way I can live here when it is done."

"Yes, Mrs, sorry, Miss Chimes."

"Thank you, Billy. I am going to look for more stuff for the library." During that time, she vanished, watched every movie possible, and bought every DVD possible.

The library was finished, and she entered the first floor and looked around; the building from a bird's eye view with the car park gave it an egg shape, with two-thirds being the library. The first floor consisted of the library being sixteen metres high with the bookshelves consisting of straight edges, creating the curve effect as they go from one side to the other; the office was at the very back. After all the furniture was added, it had a closet, desk, couch, coffee machine and a calendar. The second floor was nine metres high and with built-in projectors to create the Alternate

Reality effect of the area. She had no idea what to build on the next two floors, and the top two stories were her own house. She moved the furniture in and lived in the library from that day onwards. The roof around the living area was made of curved glass, over the area like a giant sunroof with a remote control that helps tint it to protect her from UV. Under the brick and plants, she has a bedroom and a spare room and a bathroom and an en suite. She has two stories and the biggest house. She looked up and smiled. "Hope this lasts."

For the next three years, Tana added to her collection and the books were placed on the shelves which had a blast-air wall to prevent the books from aging; she was nearly twenty-three when she got a phone call from the Louvre, and they read about her library for she has been going around collecting stories from people, including three books dating back to the fifteenth century which she collected after being passed down and donated to the library three were "Family that travelled the country" "Family of the Sword, the Line of Gladius" and "The unscathed knight". Tana listened to the owners of the Louvre and listened as the photos have been holographic for the past twenty years and that they were wondering if she could have them displayed in the library. She was delighted and travelled to Paris and went to the storage and saw all the originals hidden away; she noticed as she went down that the walls were covered with silver frames with the exact replica of the picture, but it was all a light show. She carried them and said, "Listen, I will take this to my car; I will be right back," she walked out and into the future by a second and entered the Library basement; she placed them and returned with another lot. Jumping back and forth, she soon had the whole collection; she was up to the work of Leonardo and looked at the work and then spotted one of four women and saw the name and said, "Who painted this?"

"An apprentice of Leonardo called Michelangelo Greengrass" Tana took the work and hung them around the walls; she then finished and went to her diary and read the dates she travelled to and for how long she kept a recording of her travels so she couldn't clash. When the library opened and people entered to look at the books, people questioned if these were the real deal, and Tana said, "most books are originals being kept from damage. Please remember that this library is for reading only in here; you can take an electronic copy if you wish to leave the place, but here is the only place you can actually touch a paper book." Tana saw someone watching the movie of Diana and asked, "Did she really die in a car crash?" Tana said, "The internet has been truthful since the year twenty-two hundred and newspapers were no longer used to save paper, but I can check if you wish." Tana walked out and into her office with her diary and pen and looked at her watch. She took a step into the past without hesitation or second thought and saw the crash happen. She then heard a name that she hadn't heard in seven years as she watched the ambulance take her away. "You're Marvolo Gladd, aren't you the private investigator? What are you doing in Paris?" she looked up quickly and saw a man that looked like the son of the person she saw in the drug store and realised that he was the son and vanished back into the office, she was gone for five minutes and said, "Yes, she was severely injured in a car crash and then taken to hospital and died in there." Tana wrote in her diary, "Paris, August 31st. Death of Diana"

For the next ten years, Tana collected costumes and travelled to verify the truths of books, and sounds from her audio, one of the floors had a third dimension reality which was a visit in the past, and by travelling, she verified the weather, clothing and building styles. It was approaching her thirtieth birthday when she decided to check on the so-called family that walked the country. She looked at the book's date of publication and then went to her office at the end of the gallery and grabbed the clothes that matched the time, and stepped into the past. She entered the library of Rome for London would be harder to blend in and found the book and muttered, "This can't be real. Can a man really walk around Europe" she turned and from the corner of her eye watched a man in the thirties walk over to the very same book, she decided to step back in time and entered the time that he walked and spotted the man walking in the north of the United Kingdom. Her diary filled up with dates, as she saw the battle of Hastings, the arts of the Renaissance, she had watched every movie on DVD in the basement after seeing them and buying them or in her twenties, she confirmed that Spanish Succession was in Blenheim, and twice again in Ramillies and Turin. The landing of Columbus and the first fleet, and as promised, she stepped back and drank the finest wine at the Ball of King Louis the fifteenth. Her diary was filled with facts and figures when she celebrated ten years of being open. Tana walked around her library and was about clean it up when the door opened, and a voice spoke out saying, "I am wondering if I can apply for a job. I hear you need a security guard."

The 26th Century

Mitchell arrived in Iceland in the year twenty-five hundred, and as the sun rose, he pulled off the necklace he had around his neck and took out the note and read, "To our son, if you are reading this, then you have lived a long life and are still living, remember that the Lord placed you on this earth to live for a reason, the world would have changed but you remain the same, you will be remembered but promise us you will remember the way of the Father and you will not live in pain and suffering but to the fullest, you can do, Signed your parents. Judith and Baxter." He decided to take his ship, which was docked there, to London to see how he made a difference and how to continue to do so. He headed south and arrived at the top of the United Kingdom and saw that people were acting all strange; when he arrived at the shops and asked what was happening, the keeper replied, "We lost people due to an outbreak of mutations; families have died in the past fifty years." Mitchell did not ask any more. Soon he arrived in London, only to see and remember that Diana had converted the Windsor Castle into the orphanage and foster home. It was May, and the news spread the next day that Queen George the Second passed away at age one hundred ten, people rushed in the hover trains and busses to

Buckingham Palace for the coronation of her daughter George, and Mitchell followed. When he arrived, he heard the guards shout, "The queen has been thawed; she will be with us in twenty minutes." the crowd started shouting "Queen George the Thawed!" and after twenty minutes, a thirty-year-old lady stepped out and addressed the crowd "I have being awoken from my sleep, to be informed that my mother Queen George the Second is dead, within the month I will be crowned, my husband will rule the land while I return to my sleep."

Mitchell asked the people around him, "When's the funeral?" "That is not our concern; the new queen will be crowned and then address the town on television with a speech of welcome."

Mitchell wondered what was going on; he went back to Hastings to see that every building was on stilts and everyone was friendly. He found a hotel and booked a room, he saw that the television was now just a frame and when he turned it on, it was holographic and was three dimensional, he watched a show called "The Next BIG Thing!" and after getting bored saw that half the channels were only visible if paid using credit. He went out the next day and found a cash converter machine. He went over and piled in his money from the past and, after twenty minutes, was given a drive that looked like a USB, and the screen said his total was one hundred thousand credits. He went shopping for new clothes and, after a week, found out that the coronation was on the first of June. Mitchell went to watch it, and as he was watching, a group of people came out with guns and shouted, "Death to the Royals, they took away our families." and all hell broke loose as they took aim and the Queen, Mitchell reacted fast and pulled out his staff and jumped in front of the Queen, the bullets covered him with holes and with one swipe of the staff disarmed the men. "Why do you attack the Queen?"

"Why do you protect her? She removed our freedom!"

"And how did she do that?"

"Her family signed an agreement for the doctors to experiment with giving parents DNA from animals, we became parentless when our parents died from side effects years ago, and we had no place to live since then."

Before Mitchell could open his mouth, some shouted, "Why is he still standing? He was shot with bullets?"

Mitchell realised his secret was out, so he shouted the first thing that came to his head when he was filled with emotion and memories. "I am the Immortal; I cannot die. My body survives whatever you throw at it!"

Suddenly one of the men shot Mitchell in the head, and the bullet went straight through. Mitchell stood there, and the hole in his head was seen in front of all the cameras. But with a nod, they were turned off and destroyed, and Mitchell healed and walked away as the crowd shouted, "This is impossible; the doctors could not have done this. People died when they tried, including our families!"

Mitchell fled in his boat and arrived in Russia, where he found a group of people that took him in. They were called The Underground; they were people that lost their money trying to find out the truth as to why shows needed to be bought. They were also gamblers and thugs. Mitchell lived with them and, over the radio, heard that a man had managed to recreate the formula and successfully saved his own child from dying by changing his DNA. Mitchell lived in Russia for ten years, and when he came out, the world was buzzing with news that the Queen was finally staying in charge and addressed that experimenting with DNA was banned with an alliance with RLI and would be holding a meeting with the United Nations within the next five years. Mitchell used his money and tried to find information about what he had missed, but the books were only in holographic. There were no pages and no hard copies. He couldn't find anything about the past except on the web, which was restricted. He went to get a new identity and created his birth certificate. He typed his birthday as December twelfth (year not required), for the home town he wrote down as Hastings, parents he wrote down the truth. Once done, he got an updated licence to drive every vehicle. He then decided to see if he could get a job. He went to a job agency in Moscow, and when the woman asked for his talents, Mitchell replied, "I can fight, paint, sculpture, build boats, sail, teach, fly, and did I mention survive serious bodily harm." The woman smiled and said, "Well, with that reputation, you could protect the hospital, for people are turning up demanding cures for illness; even though cancer can be cured with a tablet, people are still trying to have other illnesses cured with DNA when it was forbidden." Mitchell smiled and when to the Hospital and spent the nights in the office on the 'ground' floor, keeping watch for anyone trying to sneak in or sneak out. Mitchell watched and protected the hospital for twelve months. At the end of that, in the year twenty-five eleven, Queen George and the United Nations agreed that only successful and trialled drugs can be used to treat cancer and other life-threatening illnesses with the permission of the treated. During this time, the Amazon people were using what happened to be the DNA from their local crocodiles to make them stronger. Mitchell went on holiday around Russia that Christmas, and many people wondered who he was. The footage of his rescue was destroyed, but they could tell he was different. When twenty-five twelve came, Mitchell returned to the hospital, only to be attacked by a psych patient with a knife; getting stabbed in the back slowed down his reflexes to stop a blow to the head; he recovered in time to find the psych person robbing the place. With his staff, he stopped the patient and returned him to the cell, but when a nurse saw him remove the knife and not bleed, shouted "Mutant", Mitchell called a taxi and headed straight to China.

He arrived there in February, and on arrival, he looked around for a job, but after a week of nothing went to sleep in a hotel. The radio mentioned that children and parents have been sentenced to life in jail. The buildings were beautiful, tall and colourful; people worked on fields, in shops and in design. Mitchell looked up the past and found that since the cloud, there was an average of sixteen hundred earthquakes worldwide, killing over sixty-one thousand people a year; this stopped around twenty-four hundred when sensors in the earth's crust gave fair warning and with houses on stilts majority were saved with two hundred deaths becoming the maximum. Mitchell went back to looking for a job, and with the Chinese New Year being celebrated, Mitchell had no luck until it was the twenty-ninth, and he heard that the Olympics was back again in China last time in the year of the monkey, being placed on what they call the monkey-bars. This year it was in India; with that, Mitchell signed up as an Olympian, and after two months, it was May, and everyone was in India. The crowd was huge, with some of them being televised with two-way video. Under his real name, even though he represented China was ready. He trained during the first several events, but when it was his time to box in the ring, he heard the crowd roar when he versed his first opponent. When the man attacked, Mitchell dodged, and flashbacks of the Roman days filled his mind, he tried to shake them, but they became strong as he punched and blocked his opponents. He made it to the finals, and with the memories of his life during the eight-hundreds, he prayed, and when he lost, he smiled and mouthed, "I have lost with knowing that I didn't kill or seriously hurt them."

When he was in fencing, Mitchell began to remember the days during the wars, Hastings, Spanish, Crusades, World War and others filled his mind when he lunged and advanced, he came third overall, and when he took his medal, he thought "I won many battles, it is time I lost."

During sailing and rowing, Mitchell saw himself along with Columbus, Phillip, Bass and Flinders, even going solo around the world for Jules Verne; Mitchell rowed and sailed. He remembered diving for pearls and rowing to Antarctica as he crossed the line to make it to the final round. He thought about all the deadlines he had to come across. His teams came third and second, and during all the time, he thought, "I am no different to all of these."

His next activity was javelin, and during it, he remembered training with the aboriginals to spear for fish and wild game. His thoughts were interrupted when he saw a girl with blonde hair, and suddenly, his mind flashed back to all the encounters with the angel. He prayed, saying, "If there is an angel, then allow me to do good in the world, which seems so sad."

The last event of the Olympics, which Mitchell signed up for, was the horse event and as he rode the horse along the course remembered the times he used a horse during the wars, warning them. He came fifth, and that made him smile; he did not want to win. During the closing ceremony, Mitchell picked up a rumour of people trying to gain sight of cats for the night.

With May over, Mitchell moved to the hotel to continue to live without the fans or press. He went to the books he wrote and saw everything he had done and prayed in thanks for giving him a life. The door opened one morning in August, and the cleaner came in and said, "Any washing?" "Nope, sorry", Mitchell replied, but only to see that the cleaner had a tattoo. She smiled and said, "Hand over your money!" Mitchell realised she was a robber and pulled out his staff, the fight destroyed the room, furniture destroyed with her daggers, suddenly from the window came more people, and one said: "Sure, he is one of them, doesn't look like a Chinese Olympian?"

"Saw him on the television; he is a boxer and fencer, beware!"

Mitchell ducked as they attacked, and one came back saying, "look at what I've got" Mitchell turned to see him holding a gemstone from his collection, the rest were in the ship, which was docked, but he kept the emerald on him. "This guy has money and jewels, search him", but Mitchell dodged and got stabbed in the leg. Pulling the dagger out, they stared at his wound and said in Chinese, which Mitchell translated as "Impossible, he is not bleeding" he smiled and knocked them out, but one was still up, and with a tackle, both fell from the sixth storey towards the ground. Mitchell tossed the man into a room, pulled out his cell, and called the police before hitting the ground. The police arrived to find the phone on the ground with a message on the screen reading "sixth floor and third, room ten" Mitchell was already back in his boat recovering from broken bones, and he decided to set sail to Japan. Leaving behind a group of people that knew his secret, information was passed on, and soon it was told to a man called Xang Lei; he smiled and muttered the words, "Let the Zodiac alliance grow stronger."

In Japan, Mitchell saw the place as a city of crazy ideas. The cars and trains travelled like rollercoasters around the city, going vertical and spiralling around buildings. The towers were painted with anime, and the people were bright and cheery. Mitchell found himself a room to sleep in, he went to sleep and the next day found a directory, holographic, and read that there was a samurai school nearby. On arrival, he went up to the floor to find the master sitting there. He looked up and said, "You hold a lot of pain in your heart; coming here is unwise if you seek vengeance."

"All I seek is a way to channel my pain."

"Ok, I will teach you; first, we begin with Kendo, stick fighting."

"That I can do very well."

For four years, Mitchell trained and improved; soon, he was a master of a sword, even though he preferred the stick.

During the last year, Master spoke, "For the time I trained

you, you have grown wise but have not aged. Your eyes tell me that you lived a long time."

"More than you could imagine."

"In that case, I suggest you go and find peace, for you cannot fight with sorrow and pain like you do in your heart."

"Thank you, Sensei!"

Mitchell took his boat and sailed south towards Indonesia. He arrived after a month at sea and saw how much places change.

Mitchell walked around the island of North Maluku and saw how many people were selling and buying and living in the sky-rises. He moved to Sulawesi, where fifty per cent of the people were Christian, and the rest were Islamic. Mitchell walked around and lived in hotels, surfing and boarding as free as a bird. After a while, it was the year twenty-five seventeen, and Mitchell had got an old-fashioned letter written on synthetic paper; the message read, "I have seen you around, come to the temple on the mountain, it is time to reclaim yourself."

Unsure what to do, Mitchell followed. He arrived after a few days, and when he entered the temple, he saw a man standing next to a mirror; and when Mitchell came closer, the man said: "Mitchell Gelan, a man far older than he looks, look into the mirror and tell me what you see."

"Who are you?"

"Look, then I will talk!" the man said.

Mitchell looked into the mirror and said, "I see myself dressed in traditional Indonesian clothes. Next to a stranger."

"Look deeper; tell me who this man is staring right at you!"

Mitchell stared as the man spoke and suddenly saw himself back in Hastings, then in Rome, then in England, Italy, Spain, France, Germany, Europe, Australia, Antarctica, New Zealand, America, India, China, Egypt and Africa. Mitchell gulped and said, "I see a man that lived thousands of years, a man that made great friends, enemies and family all long gone behind him, I see a man that goes by many names, from Michel to Max, from Matthew to Midas, all to keep a secret."

"You change your name, yet keep the initials; you change identity but keep the necklace, staff and even memories."

"How do you know all this?"

"I read, I remember, I have read history and studied it, and your face keeps popping up, I am nearly one hundred and three years old, and I have learnt as much as I can, and when I saw you in the Olympics, I realised that I had to speak to you and warn you." The man coughed and then gasped, "Darn, I am getting too old; listen, people change during evolution. People wish to remain with the old times. There are organisations that keep people out of the loop and organisations that would kill to keep the old way; one of these is the Zod..." the old man coughed and then muttered, "You are the immortal; you lived through more than one era, you must stop Zod..." then the old man collapsed he was weak. Carrying him to a bed in the temple, Mitchell laid him down and then walked out of the temple, thinking, "Who was that man, what was he talking about, who are the Zod-something, and how can I help?"

Mitchell moved to Papua New Guinea and then moved to New Zealand after a few months.

Mitchell arrived in New Zealand with a warm welcome. He began to train under the name Mitchell Gelan the second for only one event: fencing. He trained and relaxed on both islands, and then when it was the year twenty-five twenty and the Olympics were held in South Africa, he travelled with the country and participated. During this time, he saw and heard that people had died due to break-ins from the top floors or muggings which had no witnesses. Mitchell participated and was fourth overall. He then walked around to watch the rest of the events and saw each country giving their all. He overheard that two hundred people had been arrested in America because of disobeying the new law, and their kids were sentenced to life in a juvenile building. Mitchell caught up with his teammates and flew back when the Olympics were over, the plane arrived back after several hours, and the Olympians celebrated the medals they had won. Mitchell decided to leave next month but was begged to stay for the next games, which would be held in New Zealand. For another four years, Mitchell stayed and trained, and when the Olympics came around, Mitchell Gelan was entering again, coming second this time.

Mitchell celebrated and then remembered as he heard around the town that robberies and arrests have been made frequent around Asia and America for disobeying the law. Mitchell was going to question them when he saw a man with a blade, running over the blade sliced into Mitchell instead of the target. Everyone stared as Mitchell pulled out the blade and said, "Was this meant for him?" the man ran away, and the police followed. Everyone stared at Mitchell as he muttered, "It's not fatal." Mitchell staggered to his boat, boarded it and sailed east towards Hawaii. That was his destination; he dodged the storms that turned the water into a wave pool, changing his direction north to rest at Tahiti. He arrived in Hawaii a month or two later; he arrived on the shores and, when the locals saw the ship docking, muttered "Déjà vu."

When they asked him in their local language, "Welcome stranger, what a fine ship, old and unique, anything that brings you here?"

Mitchell translated and replied in their local language, "I have come from New Zealand. I am a traveller; may I find a hotel and rest."

"Sure, our islands are run by thermal energy directed from the volcanoes giving us green reusable energy ever since the volcanic disaster of twenty-one eighty."

Mitchell stayed in Hawaii for about a year, and when he celebrated his two thousand twenty-fourth birthday, he asked about where to find books, remembering what the man said, "I have read about you". The locals told him about libraries that have collected books for displays, but they don't know about borrowing any books. Mitchell waited until the New Year before moving to the American coast of San Francisco. On arriving, he saw how everything had changed, the land was covered with wildlife and fauna, and the cars were hovering over the animals and the trees with ease. He found a map, looked up the local museums and libraries, and searched for his history. However, half the books were available to read, and if they were, he had to work there. Mitchell began to move around America, zigzagging around, working part-time, full time and casual in as many jobs to earn credit to travel. He ended up in Miami, Utah, Texas and Kansas more than once, and after five years, he arrived at the world-famous Smithsonian.

Entering the museum of American History, he saw that everything was automated, robotic and interactive. Screens showing events on holographic screens. Walking to the front desk, he asked if there was a job as a Security guard available.

"We do need a nightguard. The last one died with the Tyrannosaurs Rex in the Natural History Museum next door; we have three guards normally for they walk around the whole Mall."

"I will take it. Does this have access to the books?"

"You can't touch them, they are behind glass, but all books are on the resurrected old computer of the eighties to give you information from them."

"This place is like Night at the Museum, one, two and three."

"Excuse me."

"Never mind, it was before your time!"

Mitchell worked and, during the day, tried to find out about his past, but each attempt came back with the same response "Information not accessible; try another user!"

Mitchell asked after six months, "How come some information is lost?"

"That could have been when it was either stolen from the database by a hacker or bought by another museum or company!"

Mitchell continued, and soon it was nearing his birthday, and he had survived the attacks from the artefacts, which were replicas. The real ones are safe in storage. With advanced technology, Mitchell found that everything was protected, even with the Smithsonian on stilts. With Halloween around the corner, Mitchell decided to see if there were any other places and found a job needed in a library in North Dakota. According to his research, it was the world's largest library, with books available dating back to the eighteenth century. Looking up the 'Tana's Library of Historical Learning and Trivia' address, he found it in the middle of North Dakota. He retired from work after Halloween and travelled upwards towards the library. He arrived in North Dakota at Thanksgiving after sailing the boat to Canada. Resting for the holidays, he waited until his birthday and New Year's Day before heading into the museum. As he entered, he saw a woman standing behind a desk watering a tree and called out, "I am here to apply for the job as a guard!" the woman turned around and stared for a second and replied, "You sure, there is a lot of precious items in this place, as soon as one is missing, you will be fired?"

"I will take my chances."

"What are your skills?"

Mitchell rattled them off with all his jobs in the past twenty thousand years, condensing them to a small lie. The woman walked over and smiled. "You should be in the world records database; listen, give me your name and home address, and I will get back to you. My name is Tana, by the way, Tana Chimes."

"I am Mitchell Gelan, but I prefer MG; your face is familiar. Have we met before, wait a minute, Beethoven's last composing role, have you heard it?"

"Not that I am aware of; wait one minute, please, I will see if you are a trustworthy person."

Tana left, and as she did, Mitchell walked around the building. It was closed due to the fact it will be opened in February. He saw paintings of Leonardo encased in glass and protected with touch-sensitive technology. He spotted another painting, one of four women, and he walked over to the glass in shock.

Meanwhile, Tana stepped into her office and then looked at her diary; next on the list was Beethoven, questions really deaf, embarrassed to conduct again, she stepped back into time and into the crowd of people gathering to hear the music, she walked around and stopped as the music started, according to her books, he was to run away near the end, she

stood and waited when a masculine voice commented

"Heard him play before? This is my first one; I only arrived

from New Holland two years ago."

Tana replied, "Nope, this is my first time too. Shame it will be

the last one he ever conducts."

"What do you mean by that?" the man asked.

"He is deaf; I am saying it will be embarrassing if something

happens." She walked into the crowd and back into the

office, only being gone fifteen minutes. She exited the office

to see him staring at a painting. Going over, she asks, "Who

are you?"

"Where did you get this painting?" Mitchell demanded,

ignoring her.

"I will tell you once I know who you are?"

"I told you, MG!"

"As in the name of that painter?"

"WHERE DID YOU GET THIS?"

"The Louvre. When they went holographic, do you know who

painted it, and why did I just speak to you..."

"I painted it, this is mine, wait a minute" for thirty seconds

there was absolute silence and suddenly at the same time

they shouted.

"Are you immortal?"

"Are you a timewalker?"

MG asked something different, "You are the girl in this painting; how come you were in the time of Leonardo and before? Can you live forever?"

"That is me... thought she looked familiar, no, I am not immortal. I time travel. Are you saying you are immortal?"

"I cannot die. I lived for a long time, I did many things, I have seen you throughout my life."

They sat down and talked, and after ten minutes, MG got the job, and she said to him, "I will keep your secret."

"No need; the world knows, if it spreads fast enough, I survived an attack in New Zealand."

With that, they both organised the library for the New Year, talking about their powers and their adventures.

After a month of getting to know each other's gifts better, MG finally decided to see what his life did to the rest of the world and turned on the holo-top. The options appeared, and MG typed in the search engine Events that changed history and found an article about a cruise ship that crashed on the coordinates of "16.299051, -59.756470", which was southwest of Spain. MG opens the article and reads on.

"It was the eve of the fourteenth of February in the year twenty-five ten. The Ark to Paradise was a cruise ship that picked up orphans aged from sixteen to twenty-five, widows and bachelors younger than thirty-two and took them to the Bahamas, a cruise that an anonymous sponsor had paid for. It started in the year two thousand and thirty-five after a ship crashed and the captain was found in Haiti. The captain created a cruise that happened every five years, but the ship would crash around the same place on the eighth trip. This had happened twelve times when the Ark to Paradise gave off the last coordinates, and the ship went missing. The waters around that area are always calm, but for some strange reason, the water is rough on the eve of Valentine's Day. The cruise had nearly ten thousand people, all aged between seventeen and thirty-two, including the famous widow of the time called the Night Widow, and who was only twenty-one at the time and had lost four husbands. Her first….." MG stopped reading about Ebony and her husbands and called Tana.

"Tana, I need to jump into the future, to the year twenty-five fifty, to solve the cause of the crashes.

"Sorry, I rarely jump into the future that far. It is like reading the last page of a book before the middle." She looked up.

"Also, I don't know where I am going. I could end up in the middle of nowhere."

"Well, I need to find out what happens."

"I can jump you about twenty seconds into the future."

"Ok, get ready. You are taking me to these coordinates." MG walked to his room, saying, "I will be changed in a minute if you can wait that long."

Immortal and the Hex

Island of Domination

MG walked out of the room, dressed in ripped clothes and carrying an old leather satchel. "Ok, I am ready to be dropped off, so where are you going to let me go."

"I will drop you about a mile off from the location, ten seconds into the future and then leave you to find a way back; listen, what have you got considering what you read out loud and we only being together for a month."

"I think I have known you for my whole life, please!"

"Listen, I am only a person who can walk-in time. I don't even know why you want to be dropped over in the middle of nowhere."

"Those coordinates are near the West Indies. I have been there with Columbus back in the day. I know the area. If the people are lost, I can find them."

"Fine, I will drop you off, listen let me get one thing for you, only because for the last month, you and I have shared a connection of our uniqueness, and I still haven't found out anything about you in the history books, except for what I have told you."